Other books by Laurie Salzler . . .

A Kiss Before Dawn
Right Out of Nowhere
Positive Lightning
In the Stillness of Dawn

Eye of the Beholder

After
a time

Bink Books YA
Bedazzled Ink Publishing Company • Fairfield, California

978-1-943837-62-5 paperback
978-1-943837-63-2 epub
978-1-943837-23-6 mobi

Cover Design
by

Bink Books YA
a division of
Bedazzled Ink Publishing, LLC
Fairfield, California
http://www.bedazzledink.com

After A Time is dedicated to my dad, Gerry Salzler. Years ago, I amassed enough frequent flyer points to take him on a trip to the western states of the US. When I called and gave him three days to decide where he wanted to go, he was so excited and it made me smile to think I could make him that happy. However, the trip never eventuated because of circumstances neither he nor I could control.

Dad passed away in 2014, shortly after his seventy-fifth birthday. He never made it past the Pennsylvania/Ohio border. Dad, I hope your soul has traveled the world over and maybe one day when our souls meet again, we can see those sights together.

Acknowledgments

It's funny and at the same time, peculiar, how an idea for a story grows, takes hold, and then seemingly of its own accord, changes direction. This book was intended for a completely different genre than what it ended up as. But, it was a story that wanted to be written as it reads here, not as I had originally planned.

Thank you to Casey and Claudia of Bedazzled Ink for seeing the story's true form and encouraging me to continue writing it for a young adult audience.

It was a fun book to pen, and the character of Mayme (named after my Gram) was someone I would have loved to emulate back in the days of the Wild West. Thank you, Gram, wherever you are. You taught me to reach for whatever star I desired. I love and miss you deeply.

Mardi, Karen, and Cat, you Aussies kept me entertained with laughter and great conversation. You have no idea how much that helped dispel a lot of the dark stuff and make room for and encourage my creativity. I'm deeply indebted to you and value your friendship more than I could ever describe.

Leika, my Vizsla, Rainy my Jack Russell, and Kalie, my big, boofy Kelpie-cross, are my constant companions and I'm so thankful to have them in my life . . . even when they wake me up at the crack of dawn to go for walks.

Last but not least, heartfelt thanks to you, dear reader. When you picked up this book and took it home, or wherever your favorite place is to get lost in a story, you inspired me as a writer and a dreamer.

It is said that as many days as there are in the whole journey, so many are the men and horses that stand along the road, each horse and man at the interval of a day's journey; and these are stayed neither by snow nor rain nor heat nor darkness from accomplishing their appointed course with all speed.

— Herodotus, *Histories* (8.98)
(trans. A.D. God ley, 1924)

Chapter 1

"YOU STAY PUT, Mayme."

Father grasped her upper arm roughly, dragged her toward a bench, and forced her to sit down. As usual, it was easier to give in than to resist, so she plopped down like a rag doll.

He let go, gave her a look that reiterated his order to stay, and marched toward the ticket office. The suitcase lay at her feet where he'd carelessly dropped it. It held her meager belongings and she possessively slid it closer. Right now it was all she had.

She sniffed and yanked the bunched up dress from under her butt. *God, I wish I were wearing my trousers instead of this damned thing.* She silently patted herself on the back for sneaking them into her suitcase at the last minute without Mother seeing. At least she was wearing sensible shoes.

She absently ran her hand over the bench. The wood was planed smooth like glass. Every growth ring of the unfortunate tree could be seen clearly. *I wonder how many bottoms it took to sand this down.* She chewed her cheek to keep from laughing out loud at her secret joke.

She knew if she didn't find humor in such things, she'd go stark raving mad. To this day she couldn't believe how far her parent's entire charade had gone. As near as she could figure, they had cooked up a story to get rid of her once and for all. And here she was.

The big steam engine huffed twice in quick succession. A white cloud of mist engulfed her and everything around her disappeared briefly. It settled on her woolen coat and the bench. Her dark braids were jeweled with tiny drops.

A long coal box sat alongside the train. O.S.L. was painted in white on the end. It matched the letters on the train she was to board as well as the sign they'd passed on the way into the station. She assumed it stood for Oregon Short Line.

Heavy footsteps approached her from behind. "Here's your ticket." Father gruffly shoved it into her hand. "They'll tell you when to board. Somebody will meet you in Idaho to pick you up." He turned to walk away from her.

"But where in Idaho?"

"You'll get off when the train stops."

"Father, please."

He paused for a moment and without so much as a glance her way, he said over his shoulder, "You'd been warned by the school master to change your behavior. You chose to ignore him and now you have to live with the consequences. You will not be a disgrace to our family any longer."

Despite her attempt to fight the prickling behind her eyes, tears welled as she watched him walk away. She'd been discarded like trash. She dropped her chin to her chest and vowed not to let anybody see her cry. Nor would she run after him. It was quite clear what her parents thought of her. Which apparently wasn't much. She swiped the tears from her eyes and took a deep breath.

A flicker of white tickled her peripheral vision. Curious, she leaned over and discovered an open book lying halfway under the bench. The chilly breeze crinkled and slapped the pages against one another, playing haphazardly with them as she picked it up. It was well read. Or maybe very abused. She turned it over and looked at the cover. *The Adventures of Robinson Crusoe.* The book described the life of a shipwrecked man who had lived alone on an exotic island for many years. She compared the similarities of where Robinson Crusoe had found himself and where she was headed. Both unknown.

Whhhhhooooeeeooooooheeeooohh

She clutched her chest and jumped in fright. She never dreamed a train whistle could rattle her insides like that.

"All aboard!"

She took a quick look around. People were moving toward the various cars. She stood up on her tiptoes but there was no sign of her father. He hadn't changed his mind. She wadded up the ticket in her hand and took hold of the suitcase handle. She summoned her courage and walked toward the small crowd.

The second and third car filled up so she and the last ten people were ushered to the first. Once inside she tucked her suitcase under her seat and slid over to the window. She looked up and down the outside waiting area. It was now deserted except for a man dressed in a red and black formal coat.

He wore a black top hat and carried a pocket watch as he paced up and down alongside the train. He checked it several times before trotting toward the engine. Evidently it was time to go.

The iron wheels screeched beneath her. She watched as puffs of sand sprayed outward from the sides of them. Some of it had to have landed on the rails because the driving wheels finally took hold and they began to move.

Puff, puff, puff

She considered herself among the fortunate to ride in the first car. But she quickly realized luck was not the case. Her compartment was connected to the train tender, which held the coal fuel for the firebox. She knew it also held water for the boiler as she'd seen workers pumping water into it. As the train got underway, rancid puffs from the burning coal wafted into the car.

The train inched forward and strained to gain momentum. Once it had snaked its way out of the bland and grey outskirts of Chicago, she turned her attention to the interior of the car. It was decorated quite ornately. The seats were covered in pale green cloth and were supported underneath by a thick elaborately carved wooden base. The teak walls were polished to a shine and a chandelier hung from the equally glossy ceiling. It reminded her of her parent's sitting room. Up front, a wood-burning stove sat to the right of the door. The black smoke pipe extended straight up through the roof.

Clicky-clack, puff, clicky-clack, puff, clicky-clack, puff.

Every second, every repetition of the steamer wheels took her further and further away from the home she knew. She stared vacantly out the window. Her head and shoulders lulled in time with the movement of the train. Long stretches of boring barren land flew by, broken only by the appearance of a wide scattering of seemingly deserted flat board houses.

She sighed and turned her attention to the book. Despite its condition, she hoped it would provide her with a little entertainment over the miles. But it wouldn't be enough to make her forget Father's cold, unforgiving eyes when he'd shoved the ticket into her hand and wordlessly walked away without so much as a hug or goodbye.

The words on the cover swam and blurred. She rubbed at the tears that escaped and rolled down her cheeks. One dropped onto the page before she could catch it.

"Ticket please."

She blinked and looked up. A kind-faced, slender built man waited at the end of her seat. He seemed tall from where she sat, but not imposingly so. His brown hair was streaked with grey and politely slicked back. His hazel eyes held a warm friendliness that put her at ease.

"Your ticket?"

She realized she still clutched the crumpled ticket in her hand. She gave the ticket master an apologetic smile. "Sorry."

"It's quite all right, madam. Are you traveling alone?" He straightened the ball of paper and studied it.

"Yes, sir."

"Oh my dear. Eagle Rock is a long way."

"Is that in Idaho?"

"Yes, ma'am. Will you be going on from there?"

She lowered her head and tried to control the quiver of uncertainty in her voice. "I don't honestly know. Father made all the arrangements and told me to get on this train."

He smiled down at her. She read sympathy in his eyes. "My name is Clarence. If you require anything, just ask. I generally come through here once or twice an hour."

"Thank you."

"It says here that you're to have meals in the dining car."

She realized she hadn't eaten anything since breakfast and then it'd been only a piece of toast before dawn. She hadn't had much of an appetite. But now her stomach clenched in hunger at the mention of food.

She shrugged. "I guess I don't know much about that. I didn't look at the ticket."

He cocked his head. "Do you know where you're headed, child?"

"Idaho, I'm told. But that's all I know."

"Do you have family there?" She shrugged again. He narrowed his eyes. "Did you get into trouble? Are you being sent away?"

She nodded. "I got in trouble at school."

He raised his eyebrows. She knew what that particular look meant. She'd seen it many times

"Not with a boy," she said quickly.

"Ah. Something else then."

She nodded quickly, secretly hoping he didn't ask for details of her exile. When he didn't she allowed herself to relax a little. "Would it possible to get something to eat?"

He took hold of a chain that was attached to button and plucked a watch out of his breast pocket. He pried it open and stared at it intently for a few seconds. "I'm sorry. Not for a little while yet." He reached into the deep pocket of his coat and pulled out a cloth wrapped parcel. "I would offer you this though. It's not much, but at least it's something to hold you over."

"Oh no. I couldn't. But thank you." As hungry as she was and as much as she appreciated his generosity, she couldn't take this charitable man's food.

"How about half?" He smiled and she wondered if he understood her dilemma.

She deliberated for a moment and then nodded.

"You hold onto this. I'll be back for the other half once I collect the rest of the tickets." He handed it to her and winked.

He was gone before she could thank him. She quickly unwrapped it and was pleased to find a thick wedge of cheese between two slices of buttered bread. She held it in the middle so she'd be sure to only eat half. She took a bite, chewed slowly and swallowed.

She peered out the window and watched as miles of prairie went by. A small herd of pronghorns watched the train's progression from a short distance away. They didn't seem to be afraid of it, yet she assumed they were right to be wary. It appeared that all had horns, but one stood out amongst them. She wondered if he was the buck. She smiled when a fawn sprang up from the ground and disappeared behind the group. In short order they were out of sight and the landscape seemed empty again.

She looked down at her empty hand and was horrified to realize that she'd eaten the entire sandwich. A heated flush of embarrassment crept across her cheeks. Now Clarence would go hungry. Dammit. Once again she didn't think. And wasn't that what got her into trouble in the first place? She'd acted purely on impulse and didn't give a thought as to what would happen if she were to get caught.

She slid deeper into the seat and clutched her folded knees against her chest. Not quite lady-like, but she didn't give a damn. She looked out the window and wondered what kind of life she'd find in Idaho. Maybe she could get a job on a ranch and rustle cattle. She could ride well enough, but she'd have to learn how to throw a rope. Or maybe she could learn to drive a stagecoach. She smiled at the thought of galloping a team of horses over miles of uninhabited lands, transporting people to various places all over the west. Maybe if Buffalo Bill's Wild West Show came to town, she could get a job taking care of the horses. Or maybe clean Annie Oakley's guns for her. Heck, maybe she could learn to shoot as good as her and they could perform together in the show.

Endless ideas and possibilities streaked carefree through her mind like the sparks of a fire, flying every which way. The daydreams relaxed her and made her forget for a while. She rested her forehead against the window and closed her eyes. She took a deep breath and fell into a deep sleep.

Chapter 2

SHE AWOKE WITH a start. Her heart thumped wildly. *Where am I?* She frantically looked around and searched for something, anything that was familiar. There was nothing but black on the other side of the window. She glimpsed the faint line of the horizon but it appeared darker because of the brightness of the chandelier lights hanging above. Her hand came to rest on the book that lay beside her. Robinson Crusoe.

Oh. The train.

She'd been so hurt when Father walked away, abandoning her to whatever would become her. It rushed back and crashed into her chest like a horse's kick. She was sad and angry at the same time. She couldn't believe Mother had said nothing. She had just sat there with a blank glassy-eyed look on her face while Father lectured on and on about responsibility and how her actions may have tarnished the family name. The precious Watson name. She rolled her eyes. As if, God forbid. For as long as she could remember she was sure Father thought he'd hidden Mother's drinking problem. They had obviously never heard the whispers. The rumors. She had. Even her friends talked about Mother and her drunken escapades into town when Father was away. She had heard it all.

Although she missed her horse and the family mutt, she had enjoyed boarding school. And the anonymity. It'd been far enough away from home to escape all the bells and whistles, and the hell, that was associated with her prized family name. She'd had classmates whose last names were much more prominent and acclaimed than hers. And for that she was grateful. Although she'd been teased in jest about being less than a lady, she thought the other girls might have been just a bit envious. While she didn't have a care, and wanted to focus on her studies, the others had images to perfect and hue to. They'd gone to great lengths to ensure upright postures, dresses always of the finest quality, and of course, there was never ever a hair out of place on their heads.

She snorted. *They'd all seemed so fake*. Except for Mary.

Mary had been great company. She'd been able to count on seeing her, share meals and have a laugh or two. And she'd always helped Mary when she was having problems with her studies. She was a wonderful friend.

Not anymore.

One of the other passengers, a man she guessed to be about her father's age passed by, followed by a young girl. Not far behind them was a woman. She presumed she was the girl's mother.

She slid over to the edge of her seat and peered down the aisle. The family moved to the end of the car. The man opened the door next to the woodstove and helped the woman and child through to the next car.

She sighed. Although she didn't know the background of the family, she thought the little girl lucky. Wherever they were going, at least they were doing it as a family. Her throat thickened and she swallowed hard to fight the imminent tears. She rubbed her arm just to feel something.

"Hello, madam." Clarence suddenly appeared by her side. "I must apologize for not asking your name earlier."

She looked up and smiled. "It's Mayme."

"Ah, what a beautiful name."

"I, um, ate all your sandwich. I'm so sorry." She rubbed her nose to hide her renewed embarrassment.

Without a word, he reached into his pocket and removed a parcel identical to the first. He winked and said, "I always pack two just in case."

"Oh. Well thank goodness for that. But. I'm actually hungry again. Can you tell me when it's time to eat?"

"I came by to let you know just that." He offered her a kind smile and pointed in the direction the family had gone. "If you go through those doors, and into the fourth car, you'll find dinner awaiting you."

"Thank you." She got up and straightened her dress.

"Make sure you're careful going from car to car. Hold on to the railings as you step."

She nodded. "Thanks. I will."

Clarence took a step back to give her room into the aisle. "I'll stop by later to make sure you still have both your legs." He winked and smiled.

She shook her head in amusement and walked toward the door. The car swayed gently but she kept a hand on the seats nevertheless. The floor vibrated beneath her feet as she neared the door. The heavy steel wheels churned loudly on the track. She opened the door and carefully stepped out.

Her braids whipped wildly about her head and freed some errant strands. The dust smelled like the old ice in the cold box that sat in her parent's kitchen. As a youngster she loved prying the congealed water from the sides of the box.

A pang of loneliness hit her, but her stomach cried louder. She grabbed the railing and carefully stepped over the rattling joint that connected the two cars. She concentrated on not looking at the moving tracks beneath her for fear of getting motion sickness. All at once she was standing on the second car.

The sweet smell of roast beef and mashed potatoes met her as she opened the door to the fourth car. Her mouth watered and her stomach growled.

The small family that'd passed her earlier sat just inside. She looked around in dismay. All of the chairs were occupied. How would she ever be able to get a meal?

She leaned against the wall and discreetly watched her fellow passengers dine.

"Young lady!"

She looked toward the raised hand that beckoned to her.

"There's a seat over here." A lone woman sat half turned and waved for her to come over. The table she sat at was small and pressed against the wall of the car. It was no wonder she'd missed the empty seat across from the woman.

She threaded her way past the other tables. Quiet murmurs followed her as she drew closer to the woman.

"Please, sit down."

She pulled the chair out and sat down. "Thank you."

"You're very welcome. I'll enjoy the company." She extended her hand over the table. "I'm Betty Coate."

Mayme shook the offered hand. "I'm pleased to meet you Mrs. Coate."

She shook her head. "Call me Betty, please. And it's 'miss,' if you feel you need the title."

Betty's red hair was stylishly curled on top of her head. A few ringlets hung carelessly over her forehead and in front of her ears. Her red painted lips and long black eyelashes accentuated perfectly plucked eyebrows. A small mole decorated her right cheek. Her eggshell-colored dress was fashionable but not extravagant.

She heard someone tsk-tsk behind her. "My name is Mayme Watson."

Betty smiled at her. "And where do you hale from, Mayme Watson?"

She heard the tsk again and turned toward the noise.

"Don't pay any attention to them."

Mayme looked questioningly at Betty.

"Please, just take my word for it." Betty leaned over the table and whispered, "There are some on this train who are quite self-righteous. I can't be bothered with them."

"Okay. If you say so."

Betty smiled again and revealed perfect white teeth. "Now, where were we? Oh yes. You were about to tell me where you're from."

She straightened her dress and sat up straight, just as she'd been taught in school. "I'm from just outside Chicago."

"What a lovely city. I've been there a time or two. Are you traveling alone?"

"Yes. I'm going to Eagle Rock. That's in Idaho."

"Oh. Will you be meeting family there?" Betty unfolded

a napkin and placed it on her lap while a waiter filled their glasses with water.

"No. Actually, I don't really know. Father only told me I'd be met by someone at the station."

Betty furrowed her brows and sighed. "Well, I'm sure everything will work out fine."

"Are you going there as well?" She surprised herself by quickly warming to Betty. Even though she was a complete stranger, for some reason she hoped the answer was yes. She was in need of a friend.

"I'm afraid not. I'm booked to ride this iron horse all the way to San Francisco."

"Oh." Disappointment washed over her. "What will you do there?"

Betty tapped her lips with a manicured finger. "Let's just say I'll be managing a saloon of sorts."

"That sounds exciting. You'll get to meet all sorts of new people." She turned her gaze to the window and watched as vast expanses of moonlit prairie sped by. As she'd slept, a full moon had risen high in the sky. Its brightness illuminated the landscape.

She wondered how many more people were going to ask her what awaited her in Idaho. But truth be told, even she had no idea. She was scared and excited at the same time. Even though her ideas seemed elaborate, she didn't think they were completely out of the realm of possibilities for a fifteen-year-old girl. Beyond them, she couldn't imagine what her future held.

She returned her attention to Betty. "Did you always want to do that? Manage a saloon, I mean?"

"No, I can honestly say I never thought life would guide me down this path. My parents had other ideas for me when I was your age. Things changed yet again when my mother passed from consumption. I took care of Daddy until he died a few years later. He couldn't live without her I guess."

A waiter suddenly arrived with a plate in each hand.

Mayme quickly covered her lap with a napkin and stared hungrily at the food as he set a serving in front of her. Her mouth watered in anticipation of the roast beef, mashed potatoes, and corn on the cob.

"Thank you." She picked up her fork, stabbed some potatoes, and lifted it to her mouth. She realized the server was lingering. She looked on as Betty removed several bills of money from her bodice and handed it to him.

Her mouth fell open and she pressed a hand to her stomach. "Oh! I didn't realize I had to pay. I'm afraid I don't—" She set her fork down and looked at her food in dismay. Her chest tightened and she swallowed hard.

Betty waved a hand at her. "Your meals are included in the ticket price. The wait-staff expect to be tipped. Fortunately I can afford it these days. If you have your meals with me, I'd be pleased to account for you too."

"Oh no, I couldn't ask you to do that." She was aware of several sets of eyes staring in their direction. She was positive they were all focused on her. A sudden need to fade into the background and avoid notice overcame her.

Betty smiled. "You'd actually be doing me a favor by keeping me company. I'm afraid the hours between meals will be quite lonely for me as I suspect they will be for you too. Please. Allow me to do this for you."

"If you're sure." She tentatively lifted her fork.

"I'm positive. Now eat up."

AS SHE'D BEEN convinced to do, she dined with Betty for nearly every meal for the next week. There were a couple times Betty didn't show up, but the waiter always assured her that things had been taken care of. She'd wondered what had detained Betty during those times, but was polite enough to never ask, and Betty was not forthcoming with that information.

"May I ask you a question?" Betty said over lunch one day.

She shrugged and took a bite of her ham sandwich. She chewed and swallowed. "Sure."

"You don't have to answer if you think I'm being too familiar."

"Okay."

"Did you get into some sort of trouble?"

Mayme averted her eyes from Betty's gentle gaze and sighed. Was it that unusual for a young woman such as herself to be traveling alone without suspicion? Her ears and neck suddenly felt impossibly hot. Would Betty understand? She squirmed in her seat.

"I didn't think so, but my school master and parents did." She curled her toes with the admission.

"What on earth did you do?" Betty leaned over the table and whispered conspiratorially, "Did you rob a bank?"

She laughed. "No, nothing like that. They all thought I was getting too close to one of my girlfriends."

Betty raised an eyebrow. "And that caused a problem?"

"We used to stay up late studying. I got caught sleeping in her bed more than a couple times because we'd just get tired and close our eyes."

"I still don't see where that is an issue."

She looked around to make sure no one else was listening. Fortunately, the car wasn't crowded and no one sat at the tables near theirs.

"I guess it became a big deal when we got caught with our arms around each other. The house lady came in and saw Mary kiss me on the cheek." A tingling swept up the back of her neck and across her face as she recalled Mrs. Cooper's reaction. "The house lady screamed and called us both queer. After that she would sneak around trying to catch us doing something."

"How many times were you caught?"

"Four. Not counting the first time." She winced and chewed her bottom lip.

"So five times."

"Yes, ma'am." She slid deeper into her chair, awaiting the lecture that was sure to come just like every other time an adult found out what'd happened. But much to her relief, none came.

"Oh for heaven's sake. People should stop being such sticky-beaks." Betty pointed her chin at Mayme's plate and winked at her. "Eat up before your sandwich gets stale."

She nodded and took a polite bite. As she chewed she watched a well-dressed man approached their table. He wore a grey pinstriped suit over a white cotton shirt. His bow tie was tucked under his Adam's apple. As he passed, he subtly slid a small piece of paper onto the table near Betty's elbow. He glanced back at Betty and nodded slightly. Betty winked and put the paper into her bodice.

The exchange confused Mayme and she looked to Betty for an explanation. But it seemed none was forthcoming. She wondered if she should ask, and then decided she wasn't owed an answer anyway.

Chapter 3

"CLARENCE TOLD ME we'll be arriving in Eagle Rock tomorrow." She picked at her food and haphazardly moved it around the plate. She really didn't have an appetite tonight. Her stomach felt rock hard.

"You must be excited to finally get off this train." Betty sipped her coffee and then dabbed her lips with the napkin.

"Yes, I suppose I am." She put her fork down and rubbed one hand down her leg and chewed the thumbnail on the other.

"You don't sound very convincing."

"I just don't know what to expect. To be honest, I'll admit to being slightly afraid." She fidgeted further, picked up and gripped her fork so hard her knuckles went white.

"I'm sure everything will work out just fine. Despite your supposed sins, I'm sure your parents wouldn't purposely put you in a dangerous situation." Betty reached into her bodice and removed a small wad of money. She flaked off several bills and put the remainder back from where she'd gotten it. She folded the others into a small square and reached across the table with it. "Take this. It's not much. But if you find yourself in a bind, you may find you have a good use for it."

Mayme shook her head. "No, I can't take that."

Betty shook the money at her. "I won't take no for an answer. Tell you what. If in a year you find you don't need it, send it back to me."

"But how would I find you?"

Betty smiled at her compassionately. "You'd find a way. I know it."

She took the money and looked at Betty helplessly.

Betty nodded toward her bosom, indicating where she should put it.

Mayme looked around and discreetly slid it into her brassiere, which wasn't much because she had little to fill it with. “I guess that’s as safe a place as any.” A rush of warmth covered her face. She knew she wore a huge blush and gazed into her lap to hide it.

“It’s as good a place as any.” Betty chuckled. “That’s where I keep all my worldly possessions.”

Mayme realized Betty was referring to her well-endowed chest. She laughed. “I’ll keep that in mind.”

SHE WOKE EARLY and changed into her nicest dress. There was no telling what awaited her when she got off the train, but she was determined to look her very best.

She entered the dining car for breakfast and was disheartened to see her dining partner hadn’t shown up yet. Normally Betty was sipping her second cup of coffee by the time she walked in. But her chair was vacant.

She sighed and slid into her seat. A few moments later the waiter placed a plate with a slice of ham and scrambled eggs in front of her.

“Thank you. Have you seen the lady I normally eat with this morning?”

“Yes, madam. She dined very early and promptly took her leave.”

“Oh.” She tilted her chin down and frowned. “Okay. Thank you.”

“She did ask me to give you this, however.”

She looked up. He held a folded piece of paper. She took it between her thumb and index finger and mumbled, “Thanks.”

She held it in her lap until after he left. Her name was written in beautiful cursive. She unfolded it carefully and began to read:

April 8, 1886

My dearest friend Mayme,

Please forgive me for my absence at breakfast. I had full intentions of sharing a final meal and bidding you farewell, however I have unfortunately been detained. There are times we just can't control the consequences of a destiny chosen. This is one of those circumstances.

Promise me that when you disembark from this train, you will follow your dreams and not a path others have chosen for you. The west is a dangerous place, but if you have trust in yourself to move forward, you will be safe. You are a strong young lady and I hope you will eventually find someone deserving to own your love.

All the best,
Betty
p.s. Don't forget your safest asset.

She smiled sadly and carefully refolded the note. She looked around to make sure no one was watching and slipped it into her bodice. During the week she'd been traveling, Betty had made the time go faster even though they'd only seen each other at meals. Suddenly the loneliness she'd felt when she first boarded the train returned. It wasn't as if she expected Betty to hold her hand when they arrived in Eagle Rock, but her self-confidence might've been given a boost had they been able to say goodbye face-to-face.

Although she'd lost her appetite for breakfast, she discreetly wrapped the slice of ham in the napkin and slid it in next to Betty's note. She'd rather be more safe than sorry if her next meal was long in coming.

She returned to her assigned car and double-checked that she had gathered and packed everything. Satisfied, she turned her attention to the much-changed landscape outside. The dull flat prairies had transformed into rolling hills to the south and a high snow-covered mountain range to the north. The train crept up upon and eventually passed a stagecoach. Six bay horses pulled the four-wheeled coach at a hard run. White froth oozed from under their harnesses and streaked down their sweaty hides. The driver leaned forward on his bench seat, snapping the long whip above their backs, as if he was racing the iron horse.

"We'll be arriving in Eagle Rock in an hour," Clarence said from the aisle.

She turned and met his kind eyes. "Thank you. I packed early so I'm pretty sure I'm ready."

"I wish you the best of luck." He reached into his pocket and with a sly smile, removed a parcel very much like the one he'd given her the first day on the train. "I want you to take this with you. Just in case."

"Oh, Clarence. You don't have to do that." She rose from her seat and moved into the aisle.

"Do you know where you're going when we get to the train station?"

She frowned. "No. I'm afraid Father arranged everything and neglected to tell me."

"Then, please, take this. You have no idea where your next meal will come from, do you?"

She shook her head and smiled. "You are too kind. Thank you. I wish I could repay you in some way."

Clarence handed her the food and placed his other hand on top of hers as she grasped it. "Just stay safe and be well."

She nodded. "I'll do my best."

She spent the remainder of the trip scanning the landscape and glancing at the door where she hoped Betty would miraculously appear to say a proper farewell. The countryside changed but not a single soul passed through the door.

The train's whistle rose to a deafening pitch as it neared its destination. She reckoned everybody for miles knew of its impending arrival. Horse-drawn wagons and people on horseback traveled the roads in all directions. The constant traffic caused a low layer of dust to hover just above the ground.

The train slowed. Its break with momentum pushed her forward in her seat. She put her hand on the seat in front of her and braced herself. With a sudden screech of wheels, the joints of the eight cars banged together and the iron horse came to a full stop. White steam puffed out and engulfed the immediate area around the train. Once it dissipated a crowd of people suddenly came into view. Several exchanged hugs or handshakes and then lugged their baggage through the train station, where she suspected the carriages were parked on the other side.

She sighed deeply. She didn't recognize a soul and hadn't expected to. Her gut felt hollow with the uncertainty of what was to come.

She waited for the majority of people to depart before she took hold of her bag and left her seat. She took one last futile glance into the next car, searching for Betty, and stepped down onto solid ground.

Horses neighed, people yelled to one another, and dogs barked. The train puffed slowly as if recovering from a long run. The noise and commotion were nearly overwhelming. The smells of coal, horse manure, unwashed bodies, and the ever-present dust, mingled in the air. Not knowing what else to do, she sat down on a bench located near the ticket booth. From that vantage point, she hoped to catch the eye of whoever was supposed to be her porter.

Things eventually quieted as the crowd dispersed. They took their horses and dogs with them and an eerie silence settled around her. She looked around and realized she was one of only six people, and four of them were railroad workers wordlessly readying the train to continue on toward who knew where.

The men carried shovels to what looked like a short railroad car filled with coal. It was identical to the one she'd seen in Chicago except this one was attached to a hand-cranked platform so it could be moved from train to train, she suspected. In unison the men started shoveling coal into the car attached to the train.

This station was a little larger than the one in Chicago. Two other steam engines, each black and silently imposing, faced different directions on separate tracks. She briefly wondered if any of them could take her to a better place than where she was headed. She hated not knowing the plans Father had arranged for her. He could've at least told her where she was going and what she'd be doing. He'd been angry with her. There was no doubt about that. But it hardly warranted sending her this far away. She thought her parents had loved her. Apparently they loved their reputation and family name more so and had no room for a daughter they perceived as a disgrace.

"This is ridiculous. Someone must have been notified I'd be coming today." She took the suitcase by the handle and gruffly stood up. She spotted a shadowy movement in the ticket office and decided getting information from there might be her best bet.

She strode to the counter and waited a few moments. No one appeared promptly, and she knocked on the window. "Excuse me. Could somebody please help me?"

Footsteps signaled the approach of someone.

"Can I help you, young lady?" A man whom she assumed was the ticket agent, had a lean face, pitted and scarred, with very thick eyebrows. A light growth of whiskers shadowed his face. He wore a spindly pair of round wire glasses that accentuated the deep grainy circles of black under his eyes.

"I hope so. I've just arrived on this train and it appears there's no one here to meet me."

"Do you know who was supposed to greet you?"

She let out an impatient snort and crossed her arms over her chest. "I wish I did." At this point she couldn't hide her frustration, nor did she care.

He stared at her for a moment. "May I ask what your business is here?"

"I wish I knew that too. My father just handed me the ticket and didn't tell me anything." She didn't trust her mood. Another wave of irritation flowed through her. What difference did it make anyway? She felt like reaching in, grabbing the man by the shirt collar, and shaking him. But it was hardly his fault. It wasn't anyone's fault, except her own for ignoring the school headmaster's demands. She cast her eyes downward. The past continued to sneak through the back door of her thoughts. If she'd only listened she wouldn't be in this predicament. She was alone and without a single thought of where to go or what to do.

"If you walk all the way through town, you'll find a white-washed two-story house on the left. There's a sign out front that says *Waywards.* I'm pretty sure that's where you're supposed to go. Mrs. Randall runs the place. Tell her I sent you."

"Mrs. Randall? I don't understand. How can you be certain?" She blinked and shook her head slightly. She glanced around to see if there was someone else she could ask.

"Young lady, you're not the first to get off a train and not know where to go. There's been dozens of girls just like you. Now do as I say. Mrs. Randall will take good care of you." He slid the window closed and disappeared deeper into the office.

She bit her lip and gave in to the futility of it all. She needed someplace to stay. There was no getting around that fact while she figured out what she was going to do. Hopefully this Mrs. Randall would take her in.

With suitcase in hand, she walked through the station, past the hitching posts, and out onto the now deserted road. To the left was nothing but vast hummocks covered in silver prairie grass. The breeze dawdled through the stems and lazily swayed them to and fro. Large shadows moved across the steppe as clouds scudded over the blazing sun. Thermals undulated above the horizon causing a mirage-like image.

A short distance away and to the right, a row of buildings lined both sides of the road. Trees peppered the little oasis of a town, giving a green tinge against the gray sidings of the structures. She shrugged and pointed her feet in that direction. Each step raised a tiny cloud of dust that followed her. Every once in a while, the wind swirled the dust up into her nose and made her sneeze.

She stopped near the edge of where the settlement began and gathered her bearings. At first glance it seemed nearly every building had a sign in front of, or attached to it. There was a hotel on the corner and a church immediately opposite it across the street, a mercantile, saloon, livery, doctor's office, another church with a very high steeple and various houses interspersed along the street. The bawling of cattle drew her eyes to a stockade near the livery. People with indiscernible faces walked along the rutted road like ants on a mission, dodging men atop horses and numerous wagons of all sizes.

"Here goes nothing. Welcome to my future." She stiffened her shoulders, gathered her resolve, and became one of the ants.

Chapter Four

SHE ENTERED THE town and quickly scrambled to the right side of the road to avoid getting trampled by a horse. Many had the same idea and she found herself hopelessly surrounded and shuffled along at the speed of the crowd. She tried in vain to avoid colliding with shoulders and elbows, but as soon as she moved one way, she ended up bumping into another set.

She was finally deposited in front of another church as the multitude jostled her to the far edge of the street. She set her suitcase down beside her and took a deep refreshing breath, relieved to be free of the mob. The shade of the tree she found herself under was a welcome reprieve from the sun. The branches drooped to just above her head, effectively blocking out everything but the wooden cross that was shoved into the ground near her.

"Good Lord. How many churches does this place have?" She giggled and then shuddered with the thought that Father may have made arrangements to enter her into a convent. "Oh no. That's not happening." As if being too close to the church would make it so, she grabbed the suitcase and trotted across the street. She saw the *Wayward* sign just up the street.

The house was big and dazzling white where the afternoon sun touched it. But the roof was flat as if someone had shaved off the sharpest part of the peak. A big chimney protruded from the far end. Three long four-paned windows looked out onto the street. The drapes that fluttered out the open casements were yellowed with age. A small wood-planked porch flattered the front of the house around which an unkempt flower garden grew. Small nondescript weeds peeked up among the roses and marigolds. A gangly lilac bush stood proudly on the half-shaded edge of the grass.

She climbed the two steps to the threshold and set her suitcase next to the door. Hesitating briefly with her hand in the air, she adjusted her stance and knocked.

She waited what seemed an interminable amount of time before a skinny girl with fiery, chopped off red hair swung the door open. The girl wordlessly swaggered onto the porch and stopped dead still with her hands cocked on her hips. Her face was flat and rather plain. A network of freckles spanned her nose and cheeks. Her eyes were squinty and green. They moved swiftly over her, scrutinizing and sizing her up.

"Hello. I was told to see Mrs. Randall. Is she available?"

The girl sneered and squinted her eyes. "Wha fer?" Her voice was nasally and annoying even having said only two words.

"I need a place to stay."

The girl's eyes bore into Mayme like daggers. It took everything she had not to say "the hell with it," and walk away. But she needed lodging and hopefully food to go along with it.

"Don' ga no room. Y'un best gick on yer way."

"Annie? Who are you talking to? Do we have a visitor?" A woman's voice echoed from deep in the house. The hollow clunk of heels on the floorboards signaled her approach.

The redhead's eyes darted toward the entry. "Go on, now. Gick," she said quickly.

Mayme ignored the girl and focused on the woman who stood in the doorway.

"I thought I'd heard you talking to someone, Annie. Hello, I'm Mrs. Randall. Who do we have here?" She had a robust frame, was squared shouldered and strong limbed. She wasn't tall, and though stout, she was far from obese. Her face was somewhat large with a strong jaw. Her light eyebrows matched her nearly flaxen hair, which was loosely drawn into a ponytail.

Annie glared at Mayme. "I gung col 'er we gock no room an' coo be on 'er way."

Mrs. Randall took two steps toward Annie, put a hand on her shoulder and clucked. "Please forgive Annie. She's a bit mistrusting of strangers, but once she knows you, she's very loyal." She offered a reassuring smile. "I assume you've just got off the train and Mr. Heyburn sent you here."

"Yes, ma'am. I thought there'd be someone to meet me at the station, but it seems my father made that part up."

"Oh, child. I'm sorry. That happens more than I'd like to think. You need a place to stay then."

"If you have a room and it's no trouble."

Mrs. Randall slid her arm around Annie's shoulders. "Annie, please make sure the room next to yours has clean sheets and fresh water in the basin. I suspect, um, I'm sorry, I didn't ask your name."

"Mayme. Mayme Watson."

"All right, Mayme, let's get you settled. Annie, please do as I say."

Annie lowered her eyes and nodded. She walked between Mayme and Mrs. Randall and disappeared into the house.

"Would you like something to eat or drink? Annie will be busy for a few minutes. It'll give us some time to get to know each other a little."

"Thank you." She was beginning to feel more at ease despite having to acknowledge the fact that Father had essentially sent her off and abandoned her. Beneath her anger was fear. She realized then that she'd have to face it or get in touch with her fear so she'd be able to control her anger. One thing was for sure. She could not easily forgive her parents for what they'd done to her in order to save the family reputation.

She took hold of her suitcase and followed Mrs. Randall into the house. They passed a rising stairway on the right and continued down a short, dark hallway, which emptied into small but quaint kitchen.

"Please sit down. Can I get you coffee? Tea?"

"Just water would be fine." She took a seat at a square, well-used table. A vase of daisies decorated the center of the table. There was a hint of baked bread and pot roast in the air.

While Mrs. Randall poured water from a pitcher, Mayme scanned the room. An open fireplace occupied the entire back wall. Two black round-bottom pots hung above it, suspended on a long steel rod. Several pots sat on the hearth above. A wooden bench took up the majority of the adjoining wall. Sacks of flour, sugar, coffee, and other dry goods occupied one end. A rolling pin and a few hammered tin bowls were stacked nearby. A hand-cranked water pump emptied into a small sink. A collection of clean dishes dried on the bench beneath a window. She looked with curiosity at a small ladder hanging from the ceiling by twisted rope. Clumps of herbs and flowers hung upside down from it.

"Thank you," she said before taking a long swallow of water.

"You're very welcome. I see you've noticed the drying rack. The girls and I are trying our hands at an herb and vegetable garden."

"It's very unique. I've never seen anything like it." She turned to gaze at it again.

Mrs. Randall laughed. "I think you'll find there's a lot of things about my home that even the locals have never laid eyes on."

She raised her eyebrows and offered a questioning gaze. "Should I worry about that?"

"Not at all. Personally, I think you'll fit right in."

She swallowed nervously and fidgeted in her chair. "Fit into what?" Thoughts of being forced to work in a brothel or having to submit to an arranged marriage raced through her mind.

"Don't look so worried. It's nothing like you think. And before you start believing I'm a mind reader, I could tell by the look of panic on your face. I'm here to assist you in finding a life suited to a young woman such as yourself."

Mayme breathed a sigh of relief and licked her lip with cautious hope. Help was exactly what she needed. She'd landed in a foreign land, didn't know a soul, and up until now, hadn't had a smidgen of hope that things would turn out in her favor. Now she had reason to believe that everything might be all right. A sense of calm flowed over her like a silk sheet.

"What do I have to do? Whatever it is, I promise to work

hard so I can prove to you I'm worth the trouble. I got good grades in school, I'm healthy and—"

Mrs. Randall laid a hand over hers. "What I want to know is what you'd like to do with your life. Would you like to earn a wage for a while before you marry? If so, what would you like to do? There are quite a few opportunities in the area at the moment such as sewing, laundry, house cleaning, and the like. Over the next couple days, while you settle in here, I want you to think about that. Then we'll talk. In the meantime, you can help Annie with house chores. She'll show you the routine."

"Yes, ma'am." Although none of the things Mrs. Randall mentioned appealed to her in the least, she knew she might not have a choice in the matter.

"Y'un kin emmee chammer pocks," Annie announced when she entered the kitchen.

"Annie, you can't expect Mayme to clean chamber pots her first week here." Mrs. Randall patted Mayme's hand in reassurance. "Don't worry. She tries to hand that off to every newcomer."

Annie folded her arms over her flat chest and stomped her foot. "Ick ock fair. I aw 'ays haff ca goo ick."

"Yes, and you will continue to do so until you find work outside this house."

Mayme watched this exchange with some amusement. What better incentive to get a job? She wasn't sure what she'd end up doing, but she was sure Mrs. Randall would advise her on that when the time came.

"Annie, please show Mayme to her room. Breakfast and supper are both at six o'clock. There's usually no one around at lunchtime, so it's up to you to scrounge something up for yourself. If you have any questions, just come find me."

"Thank you, Mrs. Randall."

With suitcase in hand, Mayme followed Annie down the hall and up the flight of stairs. A cool breeze caressed her ankles as she climbed, but the air was noticeably warmer than downstairs.

They reached the landing and Annie paused at the top and pointed to a door to the left of the stairs. A warning of "keep owt" was chalked in large letters. "Gacks mine."

Mayme looked around and counted four more doors before her focus turned to the room Annie had walked into.

"Yers." Annie's eyes scanned the room. Then she turned on her heel and walked out.

Mayme heard a door slam behind her and assumed Annie had retreated into her own room. She stood at the entry and surveyed her accommodations. It was a clean but unadorned space with a small round rug next to a single bed. She lifted her suitcase onto it and sat down next to it. The mattress was thin and cotton-stuffed, and was covered by a thinner plain, gray woolen blanket. A chest of drawers stood against the wall. A washbasin, oil lamp, and pitcher sat on the scarred surface. A slight breeze shoved aside the flimsy curtain and allowed a ray of light to flutter in before it was blocked again.

She suddenly felt very alone. And tired. Her mind wandered back east to her parents. *Are they thinking about me? Do they even miss me?* She considered writing a letter to let them know she'd arrived safely and had found a nice caretaker. Then her anger and disappointment with what they'd done resurfaced. She hoped they felt guilty and worried about what'd happened to her. Whatever befell her, they'd not find out from her.

She removed the food parcels from her bodice and placed them on the dresser. She then opened her suitcase and unpacked. She refolded her clothes and slid them into the drawers. After sliding the suitcase under the bed, she sat down once again with the book in her hand. She flipped through the pages haphazardly. She'd read it twice on the train and never tired of it. She lay down on the bed and opened it to the first page to start it again. Robinson Crusoe had made the best of his situation. His life had become an adventure. And why couldn't she allow herself the same fate? She made a silent vow to do the same. Crusoe had not only survived the storm that had sunk his ship, but had discovered how to thrive despite all that had besieged him. She would find happiness somehow, somewhere. She made a promise that after a time she'd be dancing in the rain.

She awoke when the book slipped from her hands and onto the floor. It made an exhausted sound, like a door shutting itself at a distance. The sunlight had faded outside and long shadows darkened the majority of the room. She got to her feet and lit the oil lamp with a stick match. She adjusted the wick until the room was softly illuminated, leaving only the corners in shadows.

There was a sharp rap on her door.

"Inna."

"Thanks. I'll be right down." She poured some water into the basin and dabbed her face with the strip of cloth she'd found in the top drawer of the dresser. Then she wiped under her arms and between her legs, thinking she'd have to inquire about a bath. Feeling a bit more refreshed, she took the oil lamp and walked down the stairs.

In addition to Mrs. Randall and Annie, she was surprised to see two other girls sitting at the table. Mayme quietly joined them by sitting in the single empty chair, which was on a corner between Annie and a young woman, whom she guessed, was of Chinese decent. Her face was brown and withered like ginger root. She wore dark blue clothes and a necklace of turquoise. Her hair was gathered in pigtails.

An older girl sat on the other side of Annie. She had a narrow face partly hidden by wispy brown ringlets. Her eyes were bright behind a pair of wire spectacles. Her mouth seemed small and prim. The pale blue dress she wore was plain, but fashionable.

Mrs. Randall picked up a spoon and tapped her glass with it twice. "Girls, I'd like you to say hello to our newest resident, Mayme Watson."

"Hello, I'm Iris." The brown-haired girl craned her neck in front of Annie to see her. "That's China Polly over there."

"Iris, please be polite." Mrs. Randall gave her an admonishing look.

"What? Everybody calls her that."

"I am Lalu." Lalu shot Iris a frown and then smiled brightly at Mayme. "I am very pleased to meet you, Mayme." She bowed her head.

"It's very good to meet you as well."

"War ah you fum?" Annie said before shoveling mashed potatoes into her mouth.

"Outside of Chicago, Illinois." Mayme spooned peas onto her plate and then accepted the plate of meat from Lalu.

"You're doing well understanding Annie. Have you been around somebody without a tongue?" Iris seemed intent on taking control of the table conversation.

Mayme stopped halfway to her mouth with a forkful of meat. She shot a look at Annie and then Iris. "I, uh, no. Oh my gosh, what happened?"

"Inyuns cuck ick owck."

"I beg your pardon. Did you say Indians cut it out?" Mayme stared at Annie.

"You're good," Iris piped in.

"Annie," Mrs. Randall said. "That is hogwash."

"Eh ig! Why you ot beweeve me?" Annie slammed her palms on the table. Silverware rattled and dishes jumped. She glared at Iris. "You alays goo is." She shoved her chair back and stormed up the stairs.

A few moments later a door slammed above.

"Iris," Mrs. Randall said. "You know she's sensitive about her speech."

Iris shrugged and shoved a forkful of peas into her mouth.

Lalu had finished eating. She'd kept her head low and hadn't said a word during the exchange. "May I be excused?"

"Yes, of course. It's Iris's turn to clean up tonight."

Lalu rose and bowed to each of them before quietly shuffling out.

Mayme looked across the table and caught Mrs. Randall's eye. "Oh my God. I can't get that horrible image out of my mind."

"That's not what happened. Iris gets a bee in her bonnet

to raise dust and get Annie going." Mrs. Randall glared at Iris. "Be assured that Indians most definitely did not remove Annie's tongue."

"But how—?"

"Her father did it. She was a sickly child with frequent bouts of croup. As you can imagine, she cried a lot. Her father was a heartless drunken bastard and in a moment of rage, he took a knife to it. In between beatings, he made Dorothy, Annie's mother promise to accuse the local natives. People believed their story because at the time they'd been having problems with raids. I only found out the true story when Dorothy brought Annie to me to care for. She died two days later at the hand of her husband. Annie was eight years old by then."

"Does Annie know the truth?" Mayme felt sick to her stomach and pushed her plate away. As angry as her father was with her, she couldn't imagine him resorting to violence to cure anything.

"She has been told. The trouble is, her parents brainwashed her into thinking it was Indians no matter what anybody else said. Their descriptions of the so-called attack were so detailed that Annie believed them above all others. There is no convincing her it was all fabricated to protect her father."

"That's just horrible."

"Sad, really."

Iris rose and started clearing the table.

"Mayme, would you please help Iris tonight?" Mrs. Randall dabbed her mouth and smiled.

"Yes, of course." She pushed back from the table and picked up her plate. "I may as well jump in with both feet."

Chapter Five

MRS. RANDALL MADE a cup of hot tea, bid them good night and left them alone.

Iris gave Mayme a mischievous wink. "Want to know about China Polly?"

She shot Iris a look. "You'll get in trouble if Mrs. Randall hears."

"Rubbish." Iris scrapped the remaining meat off the plate and into the roasting pan. "Do you want to hear or not?"

Mayme carried the glasses to the sink. "You seem determined to tell me, so go ahead."

"She was a slave." Iris kept her voice low to nearly a whisper.

Mayme knew it was so Mrs. Randall wouldn't overhear.

"Don't be ridiculous. She's not colored." She scraped the plates into a tin pot.

"It doesn't matter. You'll see mostly Chinese slaves out here." Iris pumped water into a kettle and hung it over the fire to heat.

"I saw a lot of them in town. They sure don't look like slaves." Mayme tied an apron around her waist and leaned against the bench with her arms crossed. She wasn't quite sure if Iris was intent on pulling her leg or if she wanted to gossip.

"They auction them off in the livery yard when a train load comes in."

"Oh my. Those poor people."

"China Polly was one of them. By the time she was eighteen, she'd been sold four times." She ticked them off on her fingers. "By her father to a bandit for two bags of soybeans; to a Shanghai brothel; to a slave merchant of immigrants to America; and to a saloon keeper who kept prostitutes for miners."

"That poor girl. What kind of people can do that?"

Iris frowned. "It's the rich ones of course." She tossed a piece of timber onto the fire. Bright flickering sparks snapped and disappeared upward into the chimney. "The bastard figured she was getting too old, so she somehow ended up here. They made her stand naked on the auction block. When she was ordered to get dressed, she figured she'd not been purchased for a wife."

"Who bought her?"

"Mom."

"Your mother?"

"Yep. She didn't buy her for a slave of course. She just wanted help with me. My father was a logger. He died when a chain broke and a log rolled over him."

"I'm so sorry. So how did the two of you end up here?"

Iris turned and looked at her incredulously. "You don't know?"

Mayme frowned and shook her head. "Know what?"

"Mrs. Randall is my mother."

"She is? Oh. Of course, now that you say that, I do see a resemblance." She nodded quickly to hide her surprise. Truth told, she would never have guessed.

"Uh huh."

"What's that supposed to mean?"

"I don't look a thing like Mom. She always tells me I'm a spitting image of my dad. I'm not sure what that means, or if it's good or bad."

She smiled at Iris. "It means your dad was good looking."

A little while later, Mayme carried the washbasin outside to the side of the porch and poured the rinse water over the rail and onto the flowers. She returned to the kitchen and found it empty. Iris had already gone to bed. She retrieved her oil lamp and climbed the stairs to her room. She stood outside her door and tried to peer past the shadows cast by the lamp. Aside from the chirping crickets outside, not a single sound came from any of the closed doors. She turned the doorknob to her room and stepped inside. It took only a few minutes to undress, slip her nightgown over her head, and lower the wick to extinguish the light. Despite her short nap earlier, she fell asleep almost the instant her head hit the pillow.

CHIRPING BIRDS OUTSIDE the window woke her. The room was mostly dark but she recognized the shadow of the dresser. She stretched her arms over her head and immediately regretted it. Air cold enough to raise the gooseflesh on her arms lifted the drapes and wafted over her. She wrapped the blanket tighter around her and snuggled her nose into the warmth.

An abrupt knock on the door made her cringe.

"Gime goo ge' up."

"Go away. It's not even light out yet," she mumbled into her pillow.

Annie knocked harder and then again a few moments later.

"All right, all right. I'm coming." Mayme huffed and braving the cold, flung the covers back.

She hurriedly pulled on a pair of trousers to cover her bare legs. Gooseflesh peppered her skin as she doffed the gown and replaced it with a flannel shirt.

"This is just plain crazy getting up at this hour," she mumbled.

She put on thick socks and shoved her arms into a wool sweater as she slipped her feet into her shoes at the same time.

Annie's eyes widened when Mayme opened the door. Annie wordlessly looked her up and down, shook her head, and trotted down the stairs.

Thinking a cup of hot tea would help warm her up, Mayme followed close behind. She gathered her hair behind her head and fastened it in a braid as she walked.

The gray light seeping through the windows gave the stairs and entryway a ghostly appearance. The lamp light in the kitchen kept it at bay, but it wouldn't be long before it matched the sunlight outside and the lamp extinguished.

Mayme drew a deep breath beside one of the open windows. The air had a hint of dawn in it: damp and cool, metallic but not distasteful. The mountains in the near distance were framed in a pink triangle as the sun rose, gray at first, then silver, and then deep pink as the earliest sun rays caught the summits.

She entered the kitchen and conversation stopped. Mrs. Randall and Iris stared openly. Lalu glanced up briefly and bowed her head. Annie stood to the side with her arms crossed over her meager chest. She didn't look happy.

Mayme looked around at each of them. "What's the matter?"

Annie rolled her eyes and snickered before looking away.

Iris grinned but said nothing.

"Good morning, Mayme," Mrs. Randall said. "Please pardon our reaction. Your choice of clothing is rather stark for a young lady."

Mayme lifted her palms upright and looked down at her shirt and trousers. "What's the big deal? I was cold."

Iris giggled. "It's just that you look like such a boy in those clothes and with your hair back like that. I didn't recognize you at first."

"Oh." Mayme shrugged. "Well, I guess I could put on something else when it warms up." *Although it'll be something a sight more comfortable than the dress I had on yesterday.*

"That probably would be a good idea," Mrs. Randall said before taking a bite of toast. She dabbed her mouth with a napkin. "Please sit down and have some breakfast. There's hot water for tea if you'd like some."

"Yes, thank you." She slid a chair out from the table and sat next to Iris.

Iris elbowed her playfully and tittered again.

"Iris." Mrs. Randall gave her daughter a stony look.

Iris sobered and set about eating her breakfast.

"Mayme, please help Annie clean up after breakfast. I would then urge you to wander about town. Any establishments looking for help will have signs in their windows. We'll talk later about anything that may have struck your fancy."

"Is it safe? There were so many people in town yesterday, I could barely make out where I was going." Mayme poured a cup of tea and added milk until it faded to a pale tan. She helped herself to a slice of toast and spread a generous amount of butter over it.

"It's always like that, but still plenty safe. Just keep to the far sides and as close to the shops as you can. There's less likelihood of getting run over by a horse or taken in the opposite direction by the swarm of workers."

Iris and Lalu left shortly thereafter. Mrs. Randal disappeared into the bowels of the house, leaving Annie and her to put the kitchen back in order.

Annie was extremely quiet, merely grunting responses to questions Mayme asked about where to put the dishes after they'd washed them. A little later, while Annie emptied the washbasin, Mayme ducked upstairs to change.

She was anxious to explore and discover the possibilities out there. It occurred to her that it was really her first day where she had the opportunity to make decisions for herself. The train route had been predetermined and as far as could see, there'd been no alternative but to seek out Mrs. Randall. Of course there'd be some advisement from her, but Mayme was confident she'd have the final word on her job choice.

Her room had warmed up since she'd left for breakfast. She assumed it was safe to put on lighter clothing but was disinclined to wear a dress. Unfortunately she didn't have much of a choice. She'd packed plain frocks that were fashionable, but not too chic. The limited space in the suitcase was as good excuse as any to not bring any of the horrid dresses she'd been forced to wear for banquets and other venues used to promote the family name. She'd hated that and would much rather have been in trousers and shirt, and in the company of her dog and horse.

She missed both of them. Her father had purchased Abby to be a hunting dog. Her bloodlines were impeccable and she'd come from a long line of proven pointers. But she'd been afraid of gunshots from the get-go and it had taken a lot of convincing to talk Father into keeping her as a pet. Mayme wondered what would become of her. She was sure that Abby was not allowed to sleep in the house, let alone on a soft bed. If only there'd been a way to bring her along. The problem was she didn't have money to support herself, let alone a dog. Or a horse.

She wished she had Blaze now. He was her show horse and had ribboned in all the fancy jumper events. But she and Blaze had bored of all the hype. There was more exciting things to do than just ride around in a circular ring. So in between lessons and shows, they'd gone exploring. That was the one and only time she'd used the influence of her last name. The hundreds of acres surrounding the stable were used to graze and fatten cattle. She'd gone to each of the landowners and asked if she could ride on their property, dropping the Watson name at the appropriate time. She was repeatedly given permission.

She sighed with resignation. She missed the freedom of riding. Blaze hadn't care that she belonged to one of the wealthiest families in Illinois, nor what she dressed like. The times she'd spent riding or walking with Abby taught her to be comfortable with being alone. Even in the company of her parents, without a sibling, it had been a lonely upbringing. She wondered if that was what sparked her rebellious nature.

The plain blue dress was a bit faded from use. It was her favorite if she had to admit to having one. The long sleeves didn't end in lace around the wrists and there were no frills around the neckline. It would do for today.

Comfortable warmth slid over her face as she emerged from the shadow of the porch. Four vultures circled overhead, riding the thermals in search of their next meal. It was quiet at this end of town. For that she was thankful. She didn't miss the racket of the city. When she was allowed home from school she always spent the first several hours reveling in the silence.

She looked down the street and frowned. It looked like a replay of yesterday except the dust didn't seem as bad. A moving wall of people prevented her from looking past the corner shops. The crowd moved without rhyme or reason. People moved back and forth with and against each other. Every once in a while it spit out a horse and rider or a horse-drawn wagon.

Mayme kept to the right side of the road as she walked closer to the first building. She stood at the corner with her hand on the shop to appraise the surroundings. The majority of the crowd seemed to remain in the middle of the street. Like ants emerging from a nest, individuals would separate themselves from the crowd and disappear into one of the shops.

She stepped onto a makeshift walkway made of roughly hewn planks, the cracks of which were packed with dirt. From her vantage point, now above the heads of the drove, she could see that the shops were nearly identical and semidetached. Each had what looked like a path running down the side. She wondered if they were short cuts to whatever was behind them.

As she meandered down the sidewalk she often had to stop short to avoid colliding with someone going into or out of a shop. She made a mental list of the places that advertised for help: mercantile, sewing shop, bakery, butcher, and livery. She didn't think she qualified for a job at the livery because she wasn't strong enough to hoist heavy bags of grain and whatnot. She vetoed the sewing shop. She'd rather watch grass grow than have to pick up a needle and thread. Likewise, the butcher held no appeal for her either. That left the bakery and the mercantile. The thought of working in a hot shop day in and day out held no allure for her either. *That settles it. The mercantile it is.*

She knew she was supposed to discuss it with Mrs. Randall, but she'd already made her decision. Pleased with her choice, she found her way back to the mercantile, and hopefully to meet her new boss.

It wasn't hard to find. Shovels, pick axes, and other tools lined the outside wall on both sides of the door. A few dresses and an assortment of material were displayed in the window. The want ad was nailed haphazardly to the door frame and fluttered quietly in the breeze. As she passed by, she yanked it off and walked in.

It was a decent sized, dark, cozily atmospheric shop. There was a larger assortment of tools just inside. It looked like everything, including the windowsills were decorated with a light coating of dust from the road.

A few women milled about, looking at and selecting goods to place in the woven baskets held in the crook of their arms. Two stood in line to pay for their items. Mayme thought it best to wait until the man behind the counter was free before approaching him. So she wandered about. It would be a wise move on her part, she thought, to familiarize herself with the store. A row of stools sat against the counter near the huge, clear glass jars of candy. Kerosene lamps hung from the tin ceiling. The orange glow added to the shop's character. Its shelves and narrow aisles were crammed with sundries: chewing tobacco, slabs of jerky, bread, and bolts of material and other sewing supplies. A closet-sized area on the opposite side was filled with boxes of nails, more tools, and gold-panning inventory.

"Can I help you, young lady?"

Mayme looked around and realized she was now the only person in the shop, other than the shopkeeper.

He was a muscular, short man with eyes that gleamed. His voice was deep but not quite harsh. His round faced was ornamented by a handlebar moustache which stuck out quaintly under the tip of his rigid nose.

She took an easy breath, looked him directly in the eye, and stepped forward with an outstretched hand.

"I think I can help you. I'd like to apply for the open position."

He shook her hand and cocked his head. "You would, would you? Do you have any experience?"

She straightened her shoulders and held her chin high. "No. Not yet." She shot him a confident smile. "I took some business courses in school and have been well trained in etiquette. I'm a very fast learner and am sure I will become a useful asset."

"Go on. I'm listening." He crossed his arms over his chest and squinted his eyes.

Mayme leaned toward him slightly. "I can help you with your inventory presentation. For instance, if you put the boxes of nails in the order of size, customers will have an easier time finding them. And if you move the chewing tobacco away from the bread, it would be more appealing."

He huffed. "And where do you suggest I put it?"

"Well, I would move the bread away from the window so the sun doesn't cause it to stale fast. And the chewing tobacco—" She tapped her chin thoughtfully and looked around. She grinned when it came to her. "Why not on the other side of the counter with the matches and cigarette papers?"

The man frowned. He turned and stood beside her.

A wave of panic ran through Mayme. "I'm sorry if I've insulted you. I only wanted to help."

He remained silent for a moment with his gaze focused toward the counter. "What's your name?"

"My—Oh. Mayme Watson, sir."

"Okay, Mayme Watson sir. I'll try you out for a week to see how you do. The pay is two dollars a week to start." He looked at her and smiled. "You can start tomorrow morning at eight o'clock."

She pressed fingers to her smiling lips. She was overwhelmed in a good way and she felt her chest expand with self-pride. This was her first job ever and she'd gotten it without the help of anyone. Not her father or even her last name. She nodded. "Thank you, sir. I won't let you down." She rose up on her tiptoes and surveyed her place of employment.

"I'm Smart by the way."

Mayme looked at him questioningly. "Uh, so am I."

"Didn't you just say your name was Watson?"

"Sir?"

He smiled playfully. "Call me Mr. Smart. That's my last name."

"Oh. Oooh. Of course." She raised her eyebrows and giggled. "Nice to meet you, Mr. Smarty. I mean Smart."

Mr. Smart laughed heartily.

Two men walked through the doorway, one of which went straight to the counter.

"Okay, Miss Watson. I have customers to wait on. I'll see you first thing in the morning." Without waiting for a response, he strode toward the counter.

"Yes, sir. Tomorrow. I'll be here," she said to his back.

Chapter Six

MAYME RETURNED HOME and found Mrs. Randall making a cup of tea in the kitchen.

"I got a job!" She rose onto her tiptoes and bounced with excitement.

Mrs. Randall's back stiffened. She turned to face Mayme with a forced smile. "Young lady, you were supposed to consult me before you approached a business owner." She took a sip of tea and waited for a response.

Mayme pushed loose hair away from her face and bit her lower lip. "Well," she began, suddenly feeling flustered by Mrs. Randall's less-than-ideal response, "I didn't want anyone else to get it." She looked downward and shuffled her feet.

Mrs. Randall went to the table and sat down. "Have a seat and let's talk about it."

Mayme nodded hesitantly, pulled a chair out, and settled into it.

"First of all, I'm not going to reprimand you. I merely wish to explain why the rules are valid. Not every girl is right for a certain type of work, and likewise, not every type of employment suits every girl. For example, no matter what the circumstances, I wouldn't allow a young girl such as yourself to work for the local saloon. Even if the position paid well to only mop floors. It's not appropriate and certainly far from safe. I apologize for not making it clear when we spoke yesterday."

"Yes ma'am. I understand and I can assure you I did not approach the proprietor of the saloon." She took a deep breath, debating whether to explain why. In the end she decided it would be too personal of a story, not to mention accentuate the heartache she'd lived with every day since her expulsion and banishment from her home.

"Excellent. Now let's discuss your potential employment."

"Potential? No I think you misunderstood. I already accepted Mr. Smart's offer."

"Mr. Smart?" Mrs. Randall touched her throat and let out a bark of laughter. "Of the mercantile?"

"Yes. He seems very nice."

Mrs. Randall shook her head and smiled broadly. "You must've made a huge impression on him. He has resisted hiring help for the last four years."

"But he had a sign that said 'position available' taped on his window."

"And that sign has been there for four years," Mrs. Randall said over her cup of tea before taking a sip.

"I don't understand." Mayme tilted her head to one side and pursed her lips.

"It's a sad story, really." Mrs. Randall sighed and put her cup down. "Fred. Mr. Smart and his family journeyed by wagon train from Saint Louis about five years ago. Along the way a gang of criminals ambushed and overpowered the men. His wife and unborn child were trampled to death when the driver of one of the wagons tried to escape."

"Oh no. How horrible. That poor man."

"Sadly, his ten-year old daughter was also a casualty. She was killed when a bullet ricocheted off a rock and hit her while she was hiding beneath a wagon. Mr. Smart has been alone ever since."

Mayme covered her heart with a hand. "That's horrible. Did they ever catch the men who did it?"

"Yes. But seeing justice done didn't bring Mr. Smart's family back to him. I believe he's been in mourning ever since. Because of his sadness he's been reluctant to let anyone close, let alone work for him for fear it would remind him of his losses."

Mayme was speechless for a moment. To see his family killed right before his eyes was much more traumatic than what she'd been through with hers. At least she knew her parents were obviously still quite alive despite her exile and supposed inability to ever see or contact them again.

"Then why do you think he hired me?"

"Personally, I have no idea. But let's hope that you live up to whatever standards he requires. I don't know whether to advise you to tread lightly around him or just be yourself."

"Well, for me it would be easier to be myself. I mean, I was when I met him and besides, that's easier for me than to be a fake when I don't know what I'm supposed to be faking." Mayme closed her mouth and waited.

"Yes, I suppose you're right. Well, congratulations are in order then. I only have one huge requirement."

Mayme swallowed hard.

Mrs. Randall sniffed the air. "If you're going to be assisting the mercantile's customers, then I want you to smell better than them. You need a bath."

Mayme smiled with relief. "Oh, yes, please."

SHE ARRIVED OUTSIDE the mercantile the next morning, just minutes before Mr. Smart lit the lamps and unlocked the door. She was grateful she hadn't had to wait long. The morning chill peppered her arms with gooseflesh and she'd crossed them over her chest to keep warm.

"Good morning," she said as he braced the door open with a milk jug. She rubbed her arms briskly and tried not to look sensible.

"Well, that's a good sign. You showed up and made it on time." He rested his hands on his hips. "The first thing you do in the morning is put some of the tools out here. You can handle that right?"

"Yes, sir."

"Come find me when you've finished." Mr. Smart turned and disappeared inside.

She stood momentarily confused for a moment. He almost seemed displeased to see her. *I hope he hasn't had second thoughts about hiring me.* Grabbing a shovel in each hand, she began the assigned task, recalling how the tools had been arranged the previous day. She stood back and briefly admired her work before going inside.

Mr. Smart stood behind the counter, a cup of coffee in one hand and a pencil held between his thumb and index finger in the other. He tapped the pencil against his forehead twice and then scribbled something on a pad of paper.

"What would you like me to do next?"

He looked up and blinked, almost as if he'd forgotten she was there.

"Do you drink coffee?" He picked his mug up and slurped it.

"I did when my parents weren't looking. They told me it would stunt my growth and not to until I was old enough. But they never explained what they meant by old enough. I tasted my mother's one morning when she went to the toilet and decided I liked it."

Mr. Smart snorted through his nose and a hint of a smile appeared on his face. "Help yourself to a cup in the back if you want. Then I'll show you how to use the register."

The back he referred to was little more than a closet. A tiny wood-burning stove blared heat through the open doorway. The coffee pot sat on a granite warming plate with a tin mug beside it. A small pile of wood was neatly stacked next to a door she assumed led to behind the store. The only light source was from the lamp hanging just outside the room. But even in the shadowy room she could see the wrinkled photo hanging by a nail on the opposite wall.

She poured the inky liquid into the mug. As she blew over the top of it she turned and examined the picture. The light-haired woman sat on a bench and smiled toward the picture-taker. Her long white dress was tastefully spread in front of her. She wondered if it was a wedding photo.

"My wife."

Startled, she barely avoided sloshing the hot liquid onto the floor. "I'm sorry I shouldn't have—"

But Mr. Smart had already left.

She glanced at the photo and then followed him out and received the lesson on the register. It was quite easy to push the numbers in for a transaction. She'd just have to remember how to avoid getting punched in the chest when the money drawer shot out. Although the mercantile worked purely on a cash basis for the transient crowd to ensure payment, she was also instructed on how to add totals to the account book for regular customers. Since she was good at math, she found it a quite easy lesson to learn.

Before the shop opened and the first customers arrived he gave her a quick run-down on the tools. She was familiar with most of them from her work at the stable, but the gold mining supplies and a few of the farming tools were new to her. She worked hard to commit to memory all he told her, but knew she'd have questions if put on the spot.

Mr. Smart had taken her suggestions to heart and she kept busy arranging the boxes of nails in order of size and moving the chewing tobacco and bread. She'd voiced her opinion that customers would more likely buy the bread on impulse as they were checking out. Several loaves had already gone out the door.

Later that afternoon, the bell above the door rang as she moved the last of the bread loaves onto the counter. Mr. Smart had left the store to carry some heavy boxes of supplies out to a wagon for an elderly customer. It was the first time she'd been left alone in the store.

The man's face was nearly hidden by the shadow of the cowboy hat sitting low on his head. A few errant locks of blond hair sprouted out from under it. He was tall, lean, and a bit bow-legged, indicative of long hours in the saddle. A worn saddlebag hung loosely over his shoulder. His spurs jangled when his boot heels hit the wooden floor as he strode up to the counter. He removed his hat, revealing a jagged scar running from his ear to the corner of his mouth. Although Mayme couldn't begin to guess how he'd received the horrible wound, she did think he might be close to her age based on his round childish face.

"Hello," she began as she walked behind the counter. "How can I help you?"

"I need some SAA forty-fives."

Her mind raced as she tried to recall if Mr. Smart had ever mentioned the whatever-he-just-said. She knew it wasn't foodstuff, so it must be a tool of some sort.

"Uh, yes. Well, I believe you'll find them over there." She smiled and waved a hand in the direction of the tools.

"They aren't over there, missy." His blue eyes seemed to laugh at her.

She frowned at him in annoyance and then absently rubbed her cheek. She suddenly stopped, horrified that he might think she was mocking his scar. She felt the heat of a flush creep up her cheeks as she fiddled with her dress sleeves. Indecision, confusion, and embarrassment rolled into one and gathered momentum like a wind-blown tumbleweed.

"Um, are you sure?" She looked toward the door, hoping to see Mr. Smart so he could help. But the doorway remained empty. She realized she needed to buy some time until he returned. She started out from behind the counter. "I'm sure I saw them over there just this morning while I was tidying up. Let's look, shall we?"

"I'm telling you they aren't over there." He made no effort to move away from the counter.

She stopped short in front of him and placed her hands on her hips. "Well, then, why don't you tell me exactly where you think they are?"

"You work here. You should know." He flashed her a toothy grin.

Annoyed at his arrogance, she sighed heavily and clenched her jaw.

"What brings you in here, Billy?" Mr. Smart said from the doorway.

Billy winked at Mayme. "I need some bullets."

She barely refrained from growling. The idiot couldn't have just said *bullets*, could he? Of course she had no idea where they were kept. But that was beside the point.

Mr. Smart went directly behind the counter. "The usual?"

"Yes, sirree." Billy shoved his tongue into his cheek. She knew he was barely containing laughing at her.

She wanted to throw something at him. Something big. And hard.

"How long are you in town for?" Mr. Smart reached below the counter and opened a drawer Mayme hadn't noticed before. He placed a box in front of Billy. Sure enough, SSA .45 was lettered in bold ink.

Damn. Boy do I feel stupid. She averted her eyes from the bullets and pretended to focus on the account register.

"Not long I think. I quit Harrison's cattle station so I'm heading off to explore other possibilities." Billy tossed some coins onto the counter and shoved the box of bullets into the saddlebag. He placed the hat back onto his head and shoved it down. "See ya." He patted the counter once, turned, and walked toward the entrance.

"Take 'er easy out there, boy."

"It's what I do." Billy raised a hand in a backward wave and disappeared out the door.

Mr. Smart sighed and gazed after him. "He's a good boy, that one."

Mayme glanced to the front of the store and then focused on Mr. Smart. "Do you know him well?"

"As a matter of fact I do. He and his family came west the same time I did. Same wagon train." He lowered his eyes and rubbed his chin thoughtfully.

"Did his family survive the attack?"

Mr. Smart whipped his head around to stare at her.

Mayme covered her mouth. "I'm sorry. I didn't mean to bring back bad memories. It must be hard."

Mr. Smart's eyes bore into hers.

"I should just stop talking now." She broke eye contact, closed the book with a slap, and turned away.

"Wait."

Mayme stopped walking, paused, and then pivoted around. "I'm really sorry. I shouldn't have said anything."

He gave her a reassuring smile. "It's okay. It was a long time ago. Sometimes seeing Billy so grown up makes me wonder what my daughter would look like right now. Mary and Billy were the same age. My wife and I used to joke about them giving us our first grandchildren."

The prickle of tears behind her eyes made her blink hard. She had no idea what to say.

"I guess you've heard the entire story already, so there's no need for me to explain. Let's get back to work, shall we?"

"I didn't know where the bullets were kept," she said quickly.

"Ah, I must apologize for that. I knew there was something I'd forget to tell you."

"That's okay. I wouldn't know the first thing about them anyway." She scuffed her feet against the floor.

"Well, we'll have to fix that, won't we?"

"Yes, sir."

The bell above the door rang and a group of Chinese women and their children entered the store. Mr. Smart assisted the adults and Mayme kept an eye on the kids. She caught one shoving candy into his pocket and two others dipping their hands into a bag of sugar and sucking it off their fingers.

There was a steady flow of customers in and out of the mercantile for the remainder of the day. It came as quite the relief when they brought the tools in from outside, locked the door, and turned the window sign to show the store was now closed.

Mayme's feet hurt and her shoulders ached from constantly waiting on customers. It'd been a heck of a first day, but admittedly, despite being tired, she'd enjoyed herself.

Chapter Seven

"YOU MET BILLY Prescott?" Iris covered her mouth with clasped hands. "He is so handsome."

"Kik yer ooling." Annie rolled her eyes.

Mayme shrugged. "He seemed like he thought he was all that and a cup of sugar. He actually had the audacity to wink at me."

Iris gasped. "Oh, Mayme, you're so lucky. What I wouldn't give to have him even look at me."

"Oh buggar." Anne shook her head, rolled her eyes again, and then laughed.

"Oh brother is right." Mayme chuckled. "He's so arrogant, I'm surprised he can breathe with his head tipped back so far."

Annie snorted and giggled. It was the most animated Mayme had seen her. She always seemed like she was in a bad mood.

"One day you two will change your minds. I want to be married by the time I'm twenty so it's important to keep looking." Iris went back to peeling potatoes and seemed to ignore them.

Mayme glanced at Annie and rolled her eyes, which elicited a chuckle from them both.

LATER, AS MAYME lay in bed waiting to fall asleep, she thought about Iris' ambition to be married. She'd been exposed to pretty much the same mentality at boarding school. Most of the girls went there just to bide their time until an appropriate suitor came along. Then within months they'd be married and shortly after that with child.

She sighed and wondered if there was something wrong with her that she didn't share that same enthusiasm. She didn't feel peculiar. It just didn't elicit any emotions or desire to follow a path leading to courtship, marriage, and eventual child bearing. She scrunched her nose. No, she was definitely not ready for that kind of life. It was even possible she never would be. Maybe after a time.

An incoming breeze lifted the curtains and brought with it the scent of pine and the howl of a single coyote from far off. Despite her fatigue, she felt a restless stirring, as if something was calling to her. She was missing her rides on Blaze, exploring the countryside and in actuality, the serenity that accompanied it.

She rolled onto her side and pulled the blanket up to her chin. The coyote barked and howled once more. Maybe he was trying to find his place in life too.

THE WEEKS FLEW by at an amazing pace. The constant parade of customers through the mercantile door kept her and Mr. Smart on their toes and running. She wondered how he had managed before hiring her. But then she supposed he had welcomed the exhaustion at the end of the day so he could sleep soundly without the nightmares of losing his family.

When she asked about the increased business, Mr. Smart had simply replied he was sure a few new yellow veins had been discovered in the gold fields. Merchandise seemed to go out the door faster than it came in and they eventually began taking orders and simply waiting for the train to deliver the goods.

"Well, Mayme," Mr. Smart said Saturday afternoon. "It looks like we're going to have to close shop until Monday."

Mayme separated the final four bags of beans and walked to the counter. She'd been evenly spreading the various goods so it wouldn't look like the shelves were empty.

"Is that when we'll finally get the delivery we've been waiting for?"

"The supply train arrived but it won't get unloaded until sometime Monday morning."

"That's ridiculous. What's the holdup?"

"Other than the fact that railroad people suddenly

become religious on Sundays and claim a day of rest, the train was robbed."

"Oh no. Was anybody hurt?" She bounced the fingers of one hand against her lips.

"No. Not this time. They were bandits intent on stealing money. But the railroad wants to make sure nothing else was taken so they'll do a quick inventory before they unload."

"Is there anything you'd like me to do in the meantime?" She envisioned having time to herself. Since she'd started work, her days had been occupied with nothing but. Afterward, she had chores to do at the house before dropping exhausted into bed, only to start all over again the next morning.

"As a matter of fact, there is." Mr. Smart's eyes took on a mischievous twinkle. "I think it's high time you learned how to shoot."

"Really? Do you think I'm able?" She bounced on the balls of her feet.

"Young lady, in these times, I think everyone should learn how to handle a gun. Now, there are some old timers that are dead-on thinking a firearm has no place in a woman's hands. But I'm of the mind that if the women in my wagon train had been able to shoot, we might not have lost those we did." He stared at the ceiling for a moment before shaking his head as if to stop the memories Mayme had no doubt he was reliving.

She stayed silent, waiting.

"And besides," he finally said, settling his gaze on her, "I want to catch the look on some of those same old geezer's faces when they see you handling the guns and ammo with the skills of Annie Oakley."

Mayme brightened at the mention of the famous female shooter. "When can we start? Can we go now?" She swallowed a shout of glee but couldn't contain her excitement. She grinned widely and clapped her fingertips together. "Can we?"

Mr. Smart laughed. "I was thinking Sunday afternoon. I'll meet you here after lunch and you can help me load the wagon. How's that sound?"

"Perfect." She just had to figure out how she would explain her absence to her housemates.

"Oh. One other thing. Don't tell anyone what we're doing. We don't need an audience or any poo-pooing by the nay-sayers."

"Yes, sir."

Fueled by the day's events, she decided to forego her usual route home along the road. She turned the corner onto a path used mainly by delivery wagons servicing the adjoining businesses to the mercantile.

Since it was late in the afternoon and the town was nearly empty of the constant influx of miners, she had the trail to herself. Her sense of adventure pulled to her like a magnet. It'd been a while since her heart raced with possibilities of new finds.

A line of tall flowering lilacs formed a barrier between a house and the rest of town. The scent was intoxicating. She stopped and put her nose to a bunch of the fragrant flowers and breathed in the aromatic bouquet.

She looked around to make sure no one was watching, pinched a swatch off the bush, and continued on her way, frequently bringing it to her nose to sniff.

Soon she found herself wandering through prairie grass that slowly rose to her waist. She held her hand out and touched the feathery tops of the tussocks with her palm as she moved, delighting in the soft tickling.

But for the soft swishing caused by her movements, a hushed placidity surrounded her. She marveled at the quiet of the day. It was a wonderful break, leaving the noise and commotion of town behind and embracing the tranquility. But yet the perpetual silence of the evening was sometimes unnerving. During a sleepless night it was less peaceful. The bedsprings would squeak and complain from her constant tossing and turning. Her only desire was to get the repressive dark hours over with and welcome the light of day. Perhaps it was her impatience to see what the future would bring.

Mayme sidestepped the remains of a firewood pile and entered the house through a back door leading into the kitchen.

Iris and Annie sat at the kitchen table with various pieces of clothing in their laps and threaded needles between their two fingers. Iris looked up from her sewing and smiled at Mayme. Annie's brow was furrowed as she seemingly concentrated on a particular stitch.

"Hi," Mayme said as she walked by them. She went to the sink and pumped water into a glass. "What are you doing?"

Iris sighed and dropped her hands into her lap. She stretched her neck from side to side. "Drawing blood mostly. I don't mind sewing until I prick myself."

"Ow!" Annie dropped her needle and shoved the offended finger into her mouth.

"Maddie used a cork to protect her fingers." Mayme took a long swallow from her glass.

"Who's Maddie?" Iris rubbed the tips of her fingers with her thumbs.

"Oh, she was our maid."

"Ew ad a maig?" Annie's eyes grew big.

Iris swiveled around and faced Mayme. "You come from money?"

Mayme winced and slid down onto a chair. "Not anymore."

So many people she knew back east boasted of their wealth. They sported it in everything they did, said, owned, or wore. She just didn't appreciate the looks of envy like the rest of them did. More, she was embarrassed when she remembered how people like Maddie's family lived. She, along with her husband, three kids, and elderly parents lived in a tiny ramshackle house on a pig farm outside of town. The farm's owner kiddingly spouted he employed free slaves. Mayme never saw the humor in that.

"You must've done something really bad to get exiled out here," Iris said.

Mayme shrugged. She looked at the lovely stitching in Iris' lap. "Would you teach me to sew?"

"Like a dress or something?"

Annie snorted.

"No. I only want to learn to mend something. Nothing fancy." Other than not wanting to look like a total imbecile she knew it would be good value knowing how to repair something.

"Do you have something that needs fixing?" Iris clipped the thread close to the material and put the scissors back into the sewing box that sat in the middle of the table.

"Oh, as a matter of fact I do. I'll be right back." Mayme darted out of the kitchen, raced up the stairs to her room, and retrieved a dress she'd worn during her first week at work. The bottom of it had gotten caught on a plow blade and torn as she'd rushed by to wait on a customer. She had figured on replacing it at some point, but since it was a favorite of hers, she hadn't wanted to merely discard it. So she'd simply rolled it up and tucked into the back of a dresser drawer.

She soon discovered that threading the needle was the simplest part of it all. Iris showed her how to complete a couple different stitches. After nearly an hour, Mayme had succeeded in mending it. Although it was a bit of a makeshift patch, she was quite proud of having done it herself.

Annie had watched with some amusement at first, but then apparently grew bored and left, leaving Iris and Mayme alone.

"Did you really have a maid?" Iris said out of the blue.

"Yeah. She did whatever Mother didn't want to. Which was everything." Mayme refrained from commenting that her mother was usually either too drunk or too hung over to do much of anything.

"Maddie was it?"

Mayme nodded.

"Didn't Maddie teach you how to do stuff?"

Mayme shook her head. "She wasn't allowed to. Mother figured it'd be a waste of time learning something I'd never put to use."

"Because you'd someday be married and have a maid of your own." Iris frowned.

"Yes. But things change don't they?" Mayme pulled the sewing box closer to inspect the contents. There were several spools of colored threads and an assortment of needles pushed through a cloth fold.

"What's this needle used for?" Mayme pointed to a needle crudely bent into a half circle. A small piece of what looked like stained thread hung from the end of it.

"I can't believe she still has that thing." Iris pulled it out and looked at it with a mixture of disgust and wonder. "Dad put an axe into his leg once and Mom had to sew it up. She couldn't get the angle right, so she bent it like this. I guess it worked. Mom said he didn't scream as loud anyway."

"Wow. I'm not sure if I could do that." Mayme was awed by Mrs. Randall's bravery.

"I've told her that too." Iris looked up and smiled. "She just says, 'You would if you had to.'"

Mayme thought about that and decided Mrs. Randall was right. She took a deep breath. Although circumstances were different, she had already done a lot of what she'd had to. And she was sure there were even more challenges ahead.

"That's still Dad's blood on the thread," Iris said nonchalantly.

"Ew. Really?" Despite a slight feeling of revulsion, Mayme looked more closely. The thread was tinged a rusty brown. It kind of did look like old blood.

"Yep. She won't get rid of it because she says that's the last true part of Dad she still has. I sort of see her point. In a way." Iris' eyes watered a little and she quickly wiped them away.

"You still miss him." Mayme lightly touched Iris' leg and silently wished she could alleviate her pain.

Iris nodded and lowered her chin to her chest. "I really never got to know him because I was so young when he died."

"At least you know he loved you and your mother." Mayme rested a hand on Iris's shoulder. That was a similarity that she couldn't share with Iris about her own parents. She no longer knew how they felt about her. She could only imagine it was complete indifference.

"True." Iris sobered, rummaged through the sewing box and removed a cloth pouch. "Here," she said, handing it to

Mayme. "Mom made me a little sewing kit when I was small. I guess it kept me from getting into hers. You can have it."

Mayme carefully undid the three buttons holding the sack closed and looked inside. The kit consisted of two small spools of thread, one black, the other white, and two needles, one large and a much finer one. She assumed the smaller was for more delicate stitching.

She pressed fingers to her smiling lips. This gift, albeit small, filled her heart with warmth.

"Iris, I have to say this is one of the nicest things anybody has ever given me."

"You're joshing with me." Iris frowned. "Didn't you get fancy presents?"

"No, I'm not at all kidding. Most of the gifts I received from my parents afforded them bragging rights about how much it cost or how big it was. It never felt like they put much thought into what *I'd* want so it didn't seem like they were heartfelt." Mayme tapped her palm against her the left side of her chest. "This is certainly from the heart." She smiled and put her hand on Iris's shoulder again. "Thank you."

Chapter Eight

THE RAIN BEATING down on the roof Sunday morning tickled Mayme's conscious awake. She snuggled deeper into the covers, letting the sound lull her into a light doze. A low roll of thunder rumbled overhead. Her eyes flew open when she realized the significance of what she was hearing. She flung the blankets back and went to the window. Sure enough, heavy drops pelted the ground. A flash of lightning in the distance drew her eyes to the horizon, past the deep puddles already formed in the grass.

The skyline seemed brighter but she figured the chances of the weather clearing were slim. A harsh wind blew from the other side of the house, the direction from which she had no view.

She sighed with disappointment, knowing her plans were undoubtedly ruined. Since she was already up, she decided to get dressed and go downstairs. She might as well make breakfast for everybody.

There were still a few hot embers in the fireplace as she stirred the ashes. She added some thin pieces of pine timber and watched as the resin caught fire and snapped alive. She set a slightly larger slab of wood on and sparks rose sharply up the chimney. Soon the bitter smell of smoke and brewed coffee filled the room.

No sounds came from the floor above, so Mayme sat at the table and nursed a steaming cup of coffee. She'd wait a bit before adding bacon to the blackened frying pan hanging over the fire. No sense in serving cold food.

Since it was Sunday, everybody usually enjoyed a lazy morning of sleeping in. None of her housemates were churchgoers so they all were allowed to rise at their leisure. However, once the pungent aromas of breakfast wafted throughout the rest of the house, it wouldn't be long before she had company.

Mayme's stomach growled as she finished her coffee. She'd need more wood to get the fire hot enough to fry the bacon. The rain had slowed to a drizzle by the time she opened the door to fetch the wood. The cord was piled beneath an overhang next to the steps so she only had to reach out to load two logs into her arms.

In less than ten minutes time, flames rose hot on the bottom of a skillet permanently blackened from years of use. She placed the bacon on the hot surface and within seconds it hissed and crackled, releasing its sweet nutty, caramel-like smell into the house.

When it came to breakfasts, there were few aromas better than bacon sizzling and crisping in a pan. Mayme wasn't surprised to see Annie and Iris wander in, both yawning and rubbing their still sleep-filled eyes.

"You had to do it, didn't you," Iris said through a yawn.

Mayme smiled innocently. "I have no idea what you're talking about."

"Worf gan a a-arm cock." Annie walked to the sink and splashed water on her face. She rummaged through a drawer until she found a towel to scrub her face dry with.

Mayme had no idea what Annie had said. She raised her eyebrows and looked to Iris for clarification.

Iris chuckled. "Bacon is worse than an alarm clock." She put her hands on her hips and frowned. "What are you doing up so early anyway?"

"The rain woke me. I was supposed to help Mr. Smart with something today, but the rain fouled up our plans. I couldn't get back to sleep, so I decided to get up." Mayme flipped the bacon with the point of a knife, creating a new round of hissing and snapping. "It's almost ready. If someone wants to set the table, I'll fry the eggs right after."

Lalu and Mrs. Randall strolled in, one right after another and took seats at the table. They all thanked Mayme profusely for her impromptu morning meal.

By the time they finished eating, the rain had completely stopped. Renewed hope and excitement blossomed in Mayme's chest. She bit down on a smile, not wanting to raise questions from the others. Mr. Smart had asked her to keep mum about their plans and she was intent on honoring his request.

"I'll clean up," Mayme said as she slid back from the table and gathered her plate and utensils.

"No, Lalu and I will take care of the dishes and Iris and Annie will clean up the kitchen." Mrs. Randall sipped her coffee. "You're off the hook for any more chores today. It's our thanks for waking up to a wonderful breakfast."

"I don't mind." Mayme put her dishes in the sink and leaned against the counter. She had nothing to do but twiddle her thumbs until it was time to meet Mr. Smart at the mercantile.

"We won't take no for an answer, will we girls?"

A slight frown passed over Annie's face but she eventually joined the others in agreement.

Mayme smiled hesitantly. She didn't want to get on the wrong side of the girls. Annie especially had the ability to make her life miserable if she thought brownie points were being piled up with Mrs. Randall. She suddenly had a thought.

"In that case, I have to go to the mercantile today to help Mr. Smart anyway. I'll bring a few candy sticks home for everyone." Mayme knew she could win Annie over by appealing to her sweet tooth. The others smiled their thanks and that was the end of the discussion.

Mayme spent the next few hours biding time. She made her bed, straightened her room, changed the water in her washbasin, and refilled her oil lamp. Finally it was time to leave. She had changed into trousers and a long sleeved blouse. If anyone asked about her attire she'd fib and tell them she would be taking inventory and cleaning the mercantile before the new supplies arrived. Fortunately she was able to sneak out the back without notice. She retraced her steps through the field. The sun had come out and helped the wind dry the grasses through which she walked. The ground still squished beneath her feet, but it wasn't as muddy as if she had taken the road. The water filled ruts from the constant use made it nearly un-navigable to those on foot. More than one customer had come limping into the store with a turned ankle.

Mayme sat on the back step of the mercantile. There was no one else around as the businesses were closed on Sundays and most people had gone home after church to have their afternoon meal. The saloon would open much later though. Then throngs of men would wander into town to have their grog or play cards.

She didn't have to wait long before the jangle of a harness and creak of a wagon signaled her boss's arrival. A heavily muscled, but obviously older horse harnessed to a four-wheeled buckboard rounded the corner. His once sleek bay hide had flecks of gray in it, especially around his hairy muzzle.

Mr. Smart brought the horse to a halt, tipped his hat, and smiled.

"I was afraid the rain would've put you off completely. I'm pleased to see you're made of hardy stock." He set the brake, wrapped the reins around it, and stood up.

"I used to ride in the rain. It doesn't bother me. But I wondered how it would affect the guns if it rained."

"Well," Mr. Smart said as he stepped down. "While they'll work, there's no use in getting them wet and having to take them apart and oil them down. We'll have to clean the barrels when we're done, though that's not a hard job."

"Barrels?"

Mr. Smart laughed. "I guess I have my work cut out for me. This will be a lot of fun." He pulled a key ring from his pocket and unlocked the door.

Mayme smiled. She wondered how long it'd been since he'd been this keen on doing something. In the short time she'd known him, he'd always come across as very serious and contemplative. Actually, other than the circumstances of losing his family, she knew very little about him at all. Of course the opposite was true as well. He'd never asked any personal questions nor had she offered anything. But in defense, they'd had little time to talk much about anything other than the goings-on of the mercantile.

She followed him into the store and waited as he selected a few boxes of bullets and slid them into a sack, which he handed to her.

He rubbed his chin thoughtfully as he looked at the line of guns propped on end behind the counter. He chose another key from the ring and unlocked the padlock holding two ends of a chain together. The links were strung through the trigger guard of each gun, thereby securing them from sticky fingers. From the group, he lifted a short rifle and hefted it.

"This should do. Here you go," he said, handing it to her. "You should be able to handle this one."

While he reconnected the chain ends with the padlock, Mayme held the rifle gingerly, afraid that if she made the wrong move it might go off.

Mr. Smart must've seen her trepidation as he turned to her. "Don't worry. It's not loaded."

She looked at him with a combination of dread and fear. Gone was the excitement she'd felt before. She had no idea where it went. It'd merely dissipated. The notion of learning how to shoot seemed better than actually holding the gun. And she hadn't even fired it yet.

"Have you changed your mind about this?" Mr. Smart gave her a sympathetic look. "It's all right. Handling a gun isn't for everyone. Even some men can't do it, so I don't expect all women to be comfortable with one in their hands."

Mayme narrowed her eyes at him. "That sounds more like a challenge than a way out."

Mr. Smart shrugged. The twitch in the corner of his mouth and the twinkle in his eyes confirmed her suspicion.

She handed him the sack of bullets. "A woman shouldn't have to carry everything." She turned quickly and headed toward the door, hoping she looked more confident than she felt.

Once settled into the wagon, Mr. Smart released the wagon

brake and clucked to the horse. The bay tossed his head and leaned into the harness. They turned right and drove through the middle of the deserted town, carefully avoiding the biggest ruts. It was bumpy enough that they didn't say anything. Mayme clenched her teeth to avoid clacking them when they hit the bumps. She could see Mr. Smart's jaw muscles working likewise to do the same.

As soon as the road smoothed out, the horse moved into an easy trot with a slight slap of the reins on his back. Mr. Smart relaxed against the back of the seat.

"He's beautiful," Mayme commented more to herself.

"He's a good old boy. He still likes his work pulling a wagon."

"Have you had him long?"

"Yeah. He was my wife's."

"Oh." Mayme was at a loss for words.

"I had six oxen pulling the wagon coming out here. When one of them needed a break, I used to hitch him to the front for a while. He loved it. That's why my daughter named him Ox. He's the last of the stock that came west with me. I'm pretty fond of the old bugger."

Mayme hid the surprise she felt at his admission. It warmed her that he felt comfortable enough to speak candidly, but also saddened her to think he probably didn't have anyone to talk to. With that in mind, she decided to encourage conversation.

"Does he have draft blood in him?"

Mr. Smart looked at her with raised eyebrows. "Know something about horses, do you?"

"Yes, sir. I had one of my own and also did a lot of reading when I wasn't at the stable." Reading was one way she'd used to stay out from underfoot when her mother was in the drink and her father working.

The sweet smell of horse sweat wafted back. She closed her eyes and took a deep breath, reveling in the familiar aroma. How she missed her daily visits to the stable. The stable was a place of refuge, even during nasty weather. On rainy days, or when the snow was too deep to ride through, she'd haul her saddle into Blaze's stall and clean it while he munched his hay.

"Ox's dam was a Clydesdale and his sire was some rangy quarter horse that broke through a fence one night."

"That explains his big bones and heavy muscling."

Ox snorted and tossed his head.

"I think he agrees with you." Mr. Smart jiggled the reins over the horse's back. "You quit eavesdropping up there, you hear?"

Ox flicked his tail and they both laughed.

"Do you have any other stock?" Mayme half turned in her seat.

"Sure do. I have a Hereford steer that'll die of old age and a milk cow. As far as horses go, I've got a small herd of Appaloosas that roam the property."

"Those are the ones the Nez Perce developed, right?"

"Yes indeed. My stud is a direct descendant from a band the army captured. He's a cranky thing. Only responds to Indian words."

"Wow. Did you teach him that?"

Mr. Smart grunted. "Not quite. I think it's in his blood."

The landscape had changed significantly while they chatted. The tan prairie grasses had been taken over by large stands of cottonwood trees under which grew lusher, green foliage. The sun reflected off the white bark of the trees. Mayme shaded her eyes with one hand, wishing she had a brimmed hat.

As if reading her thoughts, Mr. Smart reached under the seat and pulled out a black fedora. He handed it to her. "Here, try this on. If you like it, you can have it. It's too small for my head."

Mayme wordlessly accepted it and planted the hat onto her head. Amazingly it was a perfect fit. Which made it wonder who its previous owner was. It wasn't worn hard, yet it appeared far from new. Regardless, it sufficed in shading her eyes from the glaring sun.

Mr. Smart glanced over and nodded. "It doesn't look half bad on you. You'll see it'll help you aim."

"Thank you."

Hoof beats, the jangle of the harness, and the creaking

of the wagon lulled her into a sense of belonging. It'd been ages since she'd been out in the company of a horse. A scent mixture of peppery cinnamon from the many ferns and the icy smell of water grew stronger as Mr. Smart directed Ox onto a well-used trail that angled into the cottonwoods. A hawk startled and took to the air from a high branch at woods edge. It screamed its annoyance as it circled overhead until it was a mere speck in the sky.

They entered a small meadow where a fast moving stream gurgled over rocks at the far end. The leaves of the cottonwoods high in the canopy sounded like rain as a soft breeze flowed through.

Mr. Smart pulled on the reins and halted Ox. He set the wagon brake and wound the leather straps around it.

"Here we are." He jumped down and quickly unhooked Ox from the wagon and unfastened the harness from him. He led the horse over to a grassy patch and turned him loose to graze.

Meanwhile Mayme crawled down and looked around in wonder at a landscape so different from where she lived in town. Just beyond the tree tops, she could make out the peaks of a few of the mountains in the distance.

"Have you ever been up there?"

"Up in the sawbucks?" Mr. Smart walked to her side. She nodded. "I went up once for a few weeks to try my hand at gold panning. I decided it was too lonely a business so I came back to town and opened up the mercantile."

"I heard you talking to a customer about the different types of pans and wondered how you knew so much about it." She slid the hat off and straightened her hair. "It sure is beautiful. Do you come here often?"

Mr. Smart slid his hands into his pockets. "If I get my chores done early enough on Sundays, me and Ox try to sneak over. He gets his fill of grass and I get to do some target shooting."

"The sound doesn't bother him?" Mayme pointed at Ox with her chin.

"Not in the least. There was a time when I thought he was deaf. But he's the one who gets the herd moving when I whistle."

Ox rose his head and stared at them as he chewed; long strands of grass disappearing into his mouth as he worked his jaw. He pricked his ears, tossed his head, and lowered it once again.

"See? He heard every word I said. Dang horse. I can't keep any secrets from him."

Mayme laughed. "Mr. Smart, you are so unlike any man I've ever met. The men back in Chicago treat their animals like beasts of burden. They get rid of them whenever they want something newer or better. The sales yard is where I got my horse. He had a bowed tendon when I first saw him. Father said it would be a waste of time trying to heal him and that I should just let him go to slaughter. I made a deal with the seller while Father was off looking at some fancy thoroughbred. Boy, he sure was mad. But he let me keep him. I think he thought I'd give up on him in short time and send him off."

"You miss your horse. I can hear it in your voice."

"He was my best friend." Mayme turned away quickly to hide the tears that prickled behind her eyes and welled.

"Why don't you go visit with Ox for a bit while I get everything set up? I know for a fact he likes hugs." Mr. Smart gave her a gentle push toward the horse.

She nodded and not wanting him to see her tears, she took a few steps before wiping her eyes.

Ox lifted his head and nickered softly as she approached him. He paused his chewing for a moment as if unsure of what was expected of him.

"Hey, big boy," Mayme said as she extended her hand.

He inhaled twice fast before snorting, leaving splats of mucous on her hand.

"Gee thanks." She wiped her hand on her pants and went to his side to stroke his neck.

Ox curled his neck around her, forcing her closer to his body.

Mayme put her forehead against his hide and luxuriated in the sweet smell of sweat and hay. She stood up on her toes and wrapped her arms around his muscular neck.

Ox didn't move a muscle, continuing to keep her against him. She slid her arms free of him and he finally straightened his neck.

She stood back and gazed into his eyes. Soft brown liquid filled his eye sockets. He showed no white around his pupils, giving him a very placid appearance. Through his eyes she could tell something of his personality. While a hard worker, he showed none of the spirit of a hotter bred horse like the thoroughbreds she'd been around.

"Ready when you are."

Mayme had been so wrapped up in Ox, she'd nearly forgotten about Mr. Smart. She gave Ox a few firm pats on his neck. "You're a gem, aren't you?"

She turned and walked away from him, but something made her stop and look back. Ox had started to follow her. He tossed his head and showed his teeth, but came no closer.

She laughed at his antics. "Caught you. You better stay here and fill your belly with this nice grass."

Ox snorted, lowered his head, and continued his grazing.

"He's a real character," she said once she joined Mr. Smart.

"That he is." Mr. Smart slid a bullet into the chamber of the small rifle and pushed the lever upward against the stock. "Okay. Let's get started." He held the rifle in the palms of his hand. "This is officially called an M1873, but most know it as a Winchester lever action. It holds fourteen bullets."

Mayme widened her eyes. "Wow. That's a lot."

"Yes it is."

She swallowed hard. "Does it have that many in it now?" Fourteen bullets. The number seemed daunting.

"Tell you what. We'll get you acquainted with it empty first." He pulled the lever down and the action opened, ejecting the bullet into the air. He skillfully caught it and slipped it into his shirt pocket. He then held the rifle out for her to take. "There's nothing in it anymore, so it can't hurt anything."

She took the rifle from him and held it just as he had, flat in her palms. But she held it away from her body like it was a snake that might strike at any moment.

"Your arms are going to get tired from holding it like that."

"I don't know how."

Mr. Smart nodded, went to the wagon, and returned with a second rifle, this one much longer. "Watch how I hold it and do as I do."

He rested the barrel in the crook of his left elbow and held the other end in the pit of his right arm.

Mayme studied his stance for a moment before repeating his movements. The rifle felt very foreign in her arms. Its weight wasn't uncomfortable. It just seemed awkward.

"Good. Now do this." He flipped the barrel up, propped it on his shoulder near his neck, and held the butt in the palm of his hand.

Mayme assumed an identical position. Cold steel pressed against her neck. She smelled the oil that coated it.

"Good. Now the next thing I want you to do is work the action."

"I beg your pardon. I have no idea what you just said."

Mr. Smart smiled. "That means to pull the lever down and then push it back in again."

"Oh." Mayme had to think for a moment about how she would accomplish this next task. She brought the barrel down and clasped it in her left hand. Then she tucked the other end under her elbow and held it against her hip. That freed her hand up to wrap her fingers around the lever, which she then pulled out and then shoved it back into its locked position.

"You're doing very well. I'm impressed. Are you beginning to feel more comfortable with it?"

She shrugged and offered a shy smile. "Well, yeah, it's not loaded."

Mr. Smart shook his head and chuckled. "I'll show you how to aim it first and then you do know we'll have to add the bullets."

Mayme took a deep breath and furrowed her brows. "I can do this."

"Yes, you can. And once you learn how to use a gun, you'll see you can do just about anything."

"Really?" A vein of confidence wound its way into her. *I can do this.*

"I'm positive. Ready?"

Mayme nodded.

"The first thing you need to perfect is your stance. If you don't have that, nothing will go right. With a bigger gun, you'd end up blown onto your bum."

Mayme giggled. "Don't want that."

"No, you don't. Especially if you're standing in a field of cactus. So stand with your legs apart. Like the distance they'd be when you're on a horse. Now point your toes in the direction you're going to shoot."

Mayme followed his instructions. She glanced down at her feet and then at Mr. Smart who nodded his approval.

"Now, this is the tricky part. You have to put the butt in the pocket of your shoulder. The recoil will be absorbed by your body."

Mayme lifted the rifle up and settled it against her shoulder. With a few minor adjustments from Mr. Smart, she practiced raising the gun up and fitting it where it belonged. After a few times it fell comfortably into place.

"Relax your neck and let your cheek fall naturally to the stock. This will help you line up the sights and aim correctly. Put your finger on the trigger and squeeze it slowly. Your aim is dependent on both these things."

Mr. Smart pulled two bullets from his pocket. "Watch me as I load mine and then you do the same." He opened the action and slipped the bullet in, with the pointed end facing the end of the barrel. After locking it in, he handed her the other bullet and looked at her expectantly.

Amazed her hands weren't shaking like before, with unhurried, relaxed movements, she loaded the gun. She adjusted her stance and aimed at the row of cans Mr. Smart had lined up on a fallen log. She rehearsed every step in her mind before executing it.

"When you're ready to squeeze the trigger, exhale slowly. Your body is at its stillest when you're at the bottom of that breath."

Mayme lowered the gun and took a couple deep breaths.

"You can do this, Mayme. You're handling the gun picture perfectly."

She barely noticed the loud gun blast as the can she aimed at popped off the log. "Oh my God! I did it!"

"Yes, you did. That was wonderful shooting. Ready for another?"

Mayme answered him by holding her hand out for another bullet. She smiled mischievously as he handed her four.

In her excitement she missed the next two times. But redeemed herself when she figured out what she'd done wrong, corrected it, and shot the remaining bullets. Both resulted in the cans flying off the log from the impact of the bullets.

Mr. Smart clapped her on the back. "You, my dear, are a natural. If I didn't know better, I'd think you were Annie Oakley's sister."

Mayme beamed.

They took turns shooting and didn't stop until they were both out of bullets.

The birds had long since fled after the first shot. The acrid sour smell of gunpowder lingered around them, masking the muskiness of the woods.

Mr. Smart looked to the sky with some concern. "It's getting late. We should pack up. I want to get you home before dark."

"Can we do this again?" Mayme leaned the gun against the wagon and bent to pick up the spent shells that littered the ground.

"I've had such a good time today, I think we should." He put two fingers to his mouth and whistled.

Ox raised his head, revealing the long grass drooping

down both sides of his mouth. He whinnied and trotted toward them.

They were on their way back to town in short order. Mayme's shoulder was a tad sore, but she was sure it wasn't too awfully bruised. The shooting had felt good, once she got over her fear, that is.

Chapter Nine

THE SUN WAS just beginning to set when Mr. Smart stopped the wagon in front of the house. Ox tossed his head and pawed the ground.

"He wants to go home, doesn't he?"

"It's his oats he wants. Spoiled bugger."

Despite his gruff voice, Mayme knew Mr. Smart adored the horse. It was plain in the careful way he behaved around Ox. He'd placed the harness on his back with care, making sure all his hair was straight, and he'd gently pried Ox's mouth open to insert the bit. But most notable were the gentle strokes and quiet murmuring Mr. Smart did when standing at Ox's head. It made her smile to know he was such a gentle man.

"See you tomorrow morning." Mayme hopped off the wagon and walked to the front where she gave Ox a kiss on the nose. "You're a very sweet boy. Mr. Smart is lucky to have you."

She trotted up to the porch and waved.

Mr. Smart tipped his hat and flapped the reins over Ox's back. The horse gathered his haunches, pushed into the harness, and moved into a trot toward the direction of home.

"WHERE HAVE YOU been all day?" Iris swung the door open with such momentum it slammed into the side of the house with a loud bang. She cringed. "Oops."

Mayme grabbed onto Iris' arm and held on. "You have no idea how much fun I had today! Mr. Smart taught me to shoot a gun. At first I was scared as heck, but, Iris, I'm good at it!" She knew she was babbling like a rushing creek but she could not contain her excitement.

"Wait. You did what? A gun? Whatever possessed you to do such a thing?" Iris frowned at her.

"Mr. Smart wanted me to learn about guns so I could do

my job better. But we had such a good time that we're going to target shoot every Sunday."

Iris looked her up and down and a slow smile crossed her face. "I've never known anyone like you, Mayme Watson."

The setting sun reflected orange and red in the windows.

"Let's watch the sun set." Mayme pulled her down to sit on the porch step. She leaned back on her elbows and stretched her legs in front of her. "It's so beautiful here."

"Seeing it through your eyes makes me realize how I take this for granted." Iris straightened her dress over her knees and reclined next to Mayme.

"Look," Mayme said, pointing skyward. "That's the North Star. Did you know that the entire sky revolves around that star? It never moves. That's why people use it to navigate."

"How do you know all this stuff? I never learned any of that in school."

"I guess it's because I've always researched stuff when I'm curious about something."

"You did good in school, didn't you?"

"I did all right. I loved science and math, but the girls' classes were different from the boys. The girls were supposed to devote themselves to learning how to cook and sew. That was extremely boring. But during science class, I'd write down questions about stuff so I'd remember to look it up in the library during study hall. It used to make me so mad at how much more the boys got to learn. It was all the cool stuff like farming, animal husbandry, and carpentry."

"You're such a tom boy." Iris shoved Mayme with her shoulder.

"No, I'm not. I'm just interested in more things than subjects that keep me in the house. I like being outside." She turned her head. "You know, I used to be so angry and sad that my parents sent me out here. But to tell you the truth, this is the best thing that could've happened to me."

"I have a hard time believing that." Iris sat up and rubbed her arms.

"No, seriously. My future, in fact, my entire life would've

been dictated by my last name. Out here, I can make my own decisions. Good or bad, right or wrong, they're my choices."

In the receding light, Mayme could make out an odd expression on Iris' face. "What?"

"I don't know what to think. Part of me is jealous you have the freedom to do all that, and the other part thinks you're completely insane to want to try. At any rate, can we go inside? I'm getting cold and your dinner probably is too."

THE NEXT SIX days flew by at warp speed. The mercantile was so busy with new sales and customers picking up backorders that neither Mayme nor Mr. Smart had energy at the end of the day to say anything other than a bid goodnight.

When she arrived home each night, Mayme ate dinner and then went to bed. She was asleep before her head hit the pillow.

Business slowed to a more manageable pace by Friday, and she found the stamina to relax in a hot bath after dinner.

Mayme finished washing her hair, and she heard a knock on the door. She slid deeper into the bathtub so only her neck and head were above the soapy water.

"Come in." She rubbed a sponge over her arm.

Mrs. Randall opened the door and stuck her head in. "Mayme, may we have a word?"

"Is there something wrong?" She sat up quickly. Water sloshed over the sides of the tub and pooled at the clawed feet.

"Nothing serious." Mrs. Randall slipped through the doorway and closed the door behind her. She scooted the three-legged stool next to the bathtub and sat down. "I'm concerned you're working too hard at the mercantile. You've lost weight and have been very quiet as of late. Is Mr. Smart treating you fairly?"

Mayme leaned back into the water. "I have to admit, it's been crazy busy at work. Mr. Smart is probably much more tired than I am at the end of the day. He's a very nice man by the way. There's really no need to worry."

"Are you feeling well? Maybe we should have a doctor check you over."

"Whatever for?" Mayme cocked her head.

"Darling girl, in case you haven't noticed, your clothes hang on you like a ragamuffin. A young woman should maintain a certain plumpness about her. It shows off her figure, if you know what I mean."

Mayme was aware she had slimmed down, but with all the work she'd also tightened up muscles. She figured she was stronger than she'd ever been. Even when she'd been going to the stables on a daily basis, the work she was allowed to do didn't compare to what she was involved in now.

"I feel fine, Mrs. Randall. Honest. I'm happy with how I look." She glanced at her arms. The muscles stood out without flexing and she had to admit she was quite proud of them.

"Well, you shouldn't be. My lord, your breasts are nothing but small mounds with a cherry pit planted on top. You can't possibly expect a man to be attracted to someone who resembles more a boy than a girl."

Mayme conscientiously crossed her arms over her chest and met Mrs. Randall's eyes. "When I first came here, you gave me the impression that acquiring a job and becoming my own person was a priority. I get the feeling you're trying to marry me off now. Truthfully, I'm not interested in finding a husband in the immediate future." *If at all, really.*

Mrs. Randall tipped her head back and sighed with exasperation. "You are a very strong woman. Not just physically, but mentally as well. To be honest, you remind me a lot of myself when I was your age."

"Then why the interrogation?" The bath water was beginning to cool and gooseflesh peppered her shoulders and arms. But Mayme was determined to finish this conversation. She knew if she made a move to get out, Mrs. Randall would quickly excuse herself to give her privacy.

"My mother, God rest her soul, hated that I'd rather be out in the fields with my father plowing than helping her bake and learning all the basics of housekeeping. She convinced my father that I'd end up an old spinster if I kept it up."

"I don't understand."

"The thing is, she was right. When I started doing things her way, I met a wonderful man who made me happy. I want the same for you."

"I'm not ready for an existence like that. Since I've been here, I've learned to enjoy life on my terms and not my parent's. It's funny because I was just talking to Iris about that not too long ago."

"Yes. I know. My daughter idolises you, you know."

Suddenly it dawned on her. "This isn't all about me, is it? You're concerned Iris may try to emulate me."

Mrs. Randall averted her eyes. "You should get out of that cold water or you'll catch your death." She rose and, without another word, walked out the door.

Mayme shook her head. It was now clear Mrs. Randall wanted to mold Iris to her own conformations. A wave of sadness and frustration rushed over her. Iris should be allowed to become her own woman. But that wasn't for her to decide.

While she dried herself with a rough towel, she let her thoughts wander. Should she follow Mrs. Randall's advice to look and act like a girl shopping for a husband? Search for someone to take care of her? She envisioned wearing proper dresses, spending long hours in the kitchen, mending a husband's clothing. She shuddered in revulsion at the thought of sharing a bed, her body in a sweaty coupling primarily for bearing a son to carry on the family name.

No. That was not who she was or who she wanted to be. She'd have to find another way to avoid the pressures of social conformity.

SUNDAY FINALLY ARRIVED and as usual she flew through her morning chores, barely tasting the fresh bread slathered with butter that accompanied bacon and eggs.

Since their talk, Mayme had tried to appease Mrs. Randall somewhat by donning nice dresses at mealtimes and forcing herself to eat a bit more. After she excused herself from the table, she ran upstairs to change into trousers and boots, grab the hat Mr. Smart had given her, and dart out whatever door Mrs. Randall wasn't close to.

She arrived, out of breath from running and the exhilaration of anticipating the day, and found Ox and the wagon but no Mr. Smart. A wave of disappointment washed through her at the thought of being late. She'd woken before sunrise and she couldn't remember anything that would've disrupted her morning routine. Ready to apologize for her tardiness, she entered the mercantile.

She nearly collided with Mr. Smart as she walked out of the back room.

"Oh! Goodness, you surprised me."

"Good morning, Annie." Mr. Smart had taken to calling her that since their first shooting session. But only in private, of course.

"I'm so sorry I'm late."

"You're not. I got here early to organize a few things before we left."

"I see."

"I thought we'd do something different today."

Mayme furrowed her brows. "What do you have in mind?"

He shot a devilish grin her way as he walked toward the door. "You'll see."

Instead of directing the wagon through town, Mr. Smart turned the wagon in the opposite direction.

"Gee!"

Ox immediately turned right onto a dirt path Mayme hadn't noticed before.

"You're not even going to give me a little hint?"

"Nope." He shoved his hat firmly onto his hat. "Hang on." He clucked twice and Ox tossed his head and extended his stride into a ground-covering trot.

Mayme was thrown against the back of the bench. She held onto her hat with one hand and the edge of the seat with the other.

"Hey, wait a minute. The only time I've ever seen Ox so

excited is when he thinks he's heading home." She glanced at Mr. Smart who showed no clue as to where they were going.

The prairie spread out on both sides. Shadows of clouds wandered over the short grasses. A small herd of pronghorns bounded away, frightened by the rattling wagon. Their white rumps resembled huge powder puffs that acted as an alarm device to all the others in the area. Ox merely snorted at them and picked up his speed a little more.

A rustic cabin came into view as they crested a small knoll. Erected a short distance from it stood a barn with a large coral built onto it. Four wildly spotted horses, mares, Mayme assumed because of the foals at their sides, trotted to the gate to watch their arrival. The horses shared the enclosure with a cow who paid them no attention.

"This is your farm? It's beautiful." She looked in awe at the expanse of land. Surrounded on three sides by the rich grasses of the prairie, the buildings sat comfortably tucked into a U-shaped area cut into the woods.

Ox snorted and tossed his head as Mr. Smart pulled him to a halt. "Yep, this is home. For as far as your eye can see."

Mayme closed her eyes and took a deep appreciative breath. Although it was warm, she caught brief whiffs of cold air as it was forced down the mountains by the rising thermals.

"There's nothing like this back east. I could ride for days out here and never get tired of it." Once again she was hit with a feeling of nostalgia, one that nearly only now surfaced when she thought of the long hours on Blaze's back. She rubbed her arm absently to focus on something other than the thickness in her throat.

"Before I opened the store, I used to do just that. I'm not sure why, but not so much anymore. But I'm thinking that may be about to change." He slapped the reins over Ox's back. "Come on. Let's get up."

Ox needed no encouragement and lunged into a trot.

The corralled horses pranced and whinnied to their herd mate as they approached the homestead.

A loud bang echoed from within the barn followed by a deep guttural neigh.

"That'd be Cloud. He's not too fond of being stalled and separated from his mares."

"Those are his foals then?" She leaned forward to get a better look. All four foals were nearly identical in appearance. Aside from the placement of black spots on their white rumps, they sported varying shades of black from nose to flank.

"Doesn't matter what the mare looks like, Cloud stamps his offspring just like you see them. Every once in a while he lets them have a blaze, star, or a snip on their faces, but more times than not, they're solid black."

"Beautiful. Just beautiful." Mayme jumped off the wagon and walked the short distance to the coral. The mares paid her no attention. Their attention was solely on Ox. Yet the foals eyed her suspiciously from various positions around their dams. She stuck her hand through the bars and wiggled her fingers to see if she could entice any of them to approach her.

Before too long, a red-spotted mare took three steps toward Mayme. She paused briefly, nickered encouragement to the filly who'd beforehand peered from beneath her belly and advanced toward Mayme's fingers.

"That's Rooster."

"That's a funny name for a mare." Mayme turned her head and was surprised to see Mr. Smart had yet to get off the wagon. "Shouldn't I have gotten down?"

"You're fine. I wanted to see how the horses reacted to you and you to them. Some people claim to be horse savvy until they're around them. The real test will come when you meet Cloud. He's a great judge of character."

Her breath caught in her throat. "I've never been around a stallion before."

"Then you're even. Cloud has never been around a woman before." He offered a reassuring smile. "You'll be fine. I wouldn't put you in any kind of danger."

Mayme nodded and turned her attention to the mare who

wiggled her nose against her hand. The filly watched intently just out of reach.

"When Rooster was a yearling she used to take it upon herself to jump the fence early in the morning. She somehow figured out how to get the cabin door open and from there she'd whinny at me until I got up to feed her."

Mayme laughed. She scratched beneath Rooster's jowls and watched in delight as the horse closed her eyes and extended her neck forward for more.

"She's taken quite a liking to you." Mr. Smart jumped down from his seat and proceeded to unhook Ox from the wagon. He slid the harness off and draped it over the shaft.

After his bridle was removed Ox walked over to the coral. All the foals, including Rooster's filly left their dams and pushed against each other to vie for Ox's attention.

Mayme looked on in amazement. "He's like a favorite uncle."

"Yep. I have no idea why, but every foal ever born here has been totally infatuated with him. It makes weaning really easy."

A long tongue wrapped around Mayme's wrist from behind her. She turned quickly and saw the tongue was attached to the cow she'd noticed from afar. Only now she realized it was actually a very fat red steer who sported a lot of grey around his muzzle.

The steer inhaled in her scent and then shoved his tongue into his nostrils. His gray whiskers accentuated his placid appearance. Mayme knew without asking that this animal was definitely more of a pasture pet than a source of meat.

"Now that you've met Fred, let's see what Cloud thinks of you." Mr. Smart opened the door to the barn. As she followed him, he said, "And no funny remarks about Fred."

"Oh, I wouldn't dream of it," Mayme said with just a hint of sarcasm.

Mr. Smart shook his finger over his shoulder.

Mayme stifled a giggle but quickly swallowed it as a loud bang echoed throughout the barn.

The boldly spotted white head of the stallion loomed over

the stall gate. The white sclera around his eyes accentuated his attitude.

Mayme stood back from the stall. Caution more than fear, made her observe him from a distance. His thick neck sported a thin flea-bitten mane. His short back flowed into a powerful hind end.

"Where'd he get all the scars from?" If she hadn't known better, she would've sworn he'd been beaten recently. In addition to the black spots peppering his hide, there were several semi-circular gashes on his neck and rump, some barely scabbed over.

"From the damned mustang stallion. Pardon my language, but he's a bold son-of-a-gun. He comes down from the hills every so often to try and steal my mares to add to his herd. If it wasn't for Cloud here, Ox would be the only horse around here."

"Those are fight wounds?"

"Yeah. That's why he's in here and the mares corralled. He was a bloody mess this time. I figured they'd all be safer locked up while he recuperated."

"It looks like Cloud got the short end of the stick."

"Yeah. That was all my fault. While the mares fed on some oats by the barn the other day, I got working him on a long line inside the coral. The mustang snuck in, looking to drive the mares away. Cloud jumped the fence, rope and all and they got into it. The rope did him more harm than good. He got it tangled around his legs and had a hard time defending himself. By the time I got the rifle from the house, it was over with. I don't how he managed to keep that stallion from taking the mares."

"You were going to shoot him?" Mayme looked at him incredulously and touched her lips with her fingers. She couldn't imagine Mr. Smart doing such a heartless thing, especially when there was an arthritic pet steer just outside.

"Yes, I was. Here's the thing. One of these days, that stallion is going to cripple Cloud. And worse, he's going to succeed in taking those mares outside. He could ruin my horse-breeding program all in one fell swoop. Let's put it this way. If you had to choose between your Blaze and knowing that mustang ran free, what would it be?"

"Couldn't you try to catch him?"

"Many tried and none have succeeded. The bugger is just too smart. Somehow he gets to knowing somebody's after him so he hides his herd deep in the mountains."

Mayme listened with complete fascination. "Wow. Can you imagine owning a horse like that?"

"Aw, Mayme, he'd be way too dangerous and unpredictable. I'd be wary about any of his offspring. Horses like that tend to pass their errant tempers onto their foals. They can't be tamed."

Mayme inhaled deeply through her nose and exhaled it loudly through her mouth. "I'd sure be willing to try." She raised her chin and walked to Cloud's door.

Chapter Ten

MAYME HAD HER back to the counter on a quiet Wednesday afternoon. Business was finally slow enough she had the opportunity to do a little dusting, although most times it seemed futile. The front door was always open except when a storm blew in from the west. The constant traffic from the multitude of wagons and horses on the road seemed to keep a permanent cloud of dust adrift in the air. It attached itself to the mercantile patronage and was then inconveniently deposited on everything in the store as soon as they entered.

"I need some SAA forty-fives."

Mayme barely stifled a yelp and spun around. She hadn't heard the man enter. A flush of adrenaline tingled through her body. She narrowed her eyes as she realized it was none other than Billy Prescott. She walked around the counter and looked pointedly at the spurs on his boots.

She put her hands on her hips. "You snuck up on me."

Billy gave her a toothy grin, shook his head, and tapped the floor with the tip of his boot. The jangling spur taunted her. "No, ma'am. I would never do that. You just didn't wasn't paying no attention."

"Bullocks." She returned to behind the counter, opened the ammunition drawer, and tossed a box at him. "That'll be fifty cents, please." Her voice held none of the courtesy normally exhibited toward customers.

Billy flicked a couple coins in her direction. They spun like chaotic tops on the counter. "Thanks."

He tucked the bullets into his jacket pocket and from the same spot withdrew a folded piece of paper. "Is Fred around? I need to ask him something."

The back door slammed suddenly and a moment later Mr. Smart walked in with the rifle she'd been using.

Perfect timing. Now I won't have to deal with this egotistical cowboy.

"Hiya, Billy. Nice to see you back in town."

"Won't be for long. I got me a new job." He handed the paper to Mr. Smart. "My boss asked me to pass out some of these here flyers. Can you tape one up on your door?"

Mr. Smart took the paper from Billy and studied it for a few moments. He raised his eyebrows, shoved his lower lip out, and nodded. He worked his jaw and finally said, "Sounds like a great opportunity, but pretty dangerous if you ask me."

Mayme craned her neck to see what was written on the paper. Mr. Smart noticed her interest and passed it to her. "Please tack this onto the door when you're done."

Mayme nodded and read with fascination as she walked toward the entrance:

> The United States needs Postal Riders
> Wanted: Skinny, wiry fellows.
> Must be 16 years or older and use any method necessary to deliver the mail, including but not limited to horseback, boats, sled, snowshoes and skis. Orphans preferred.

With the words playing heavily on her mind, she pushed it over a nail, top and bottom, thereby securing it to the door. She retrieved her feather duster and listened discreetly as Mr. Smart and Billy continued to discuss the postal service.

"They don't supply the guns," Billy said. "But I'll be carrying a carbine and two revolvers. There's not much that can get past that."

"Depends on what kind of shot you are, doesn't it?" Mr. Smart gave him a wry smile.

Billy snorted and puffed his chest out. "You said yourself I was one of the best around."

Mr. Smart caught Mayme's eye and winked.

"What kind of route are they expecting you to ride?" Mr. Smart set the rifle into the empty spot among the other guns. "This place isn't exactly a big enough city to generate a lot of mail."

Billy leaned against the counter and hooked one leg over the other. He rubbed his chin, which had the mere beginnings of a blond scruff of beard. He jangled his spurs against each other and grinned at Mayme.

Mayme rolled her eyes and not for the first time thought him too cocky for his own good.

"That's the thing," Billy said, turning his attention back to Mr. Smart. "The postmaster wants me to ride between two main offices."

"That won't be too bad for you then. The country south of here is pretty safe, I hear."

"I'll be hauling a lot of mail. That's what'll be the most demanding. They expect the riders to meet up at scheduled times at scheduled places. That means I'll be pushing pretty hard from one drop-off to the other. Some of the routes are up into the mountains."

Mr. Smart threw his head back and laughed. "You expect that old plug gelding of yours to hold up to that? I reckon he'd pull up lame on the first day, maybe after the first hour out."

"I won't be riding Sage. The company that bought out the Pony Express is under contract to supply some of the horses. I have some money saved up to buy me one from there. I was hoping you'd be willing to look after Sage for me though. You can use him if you want."

"Hmm. Are you sure you want to do something like this?"

Billy shook his head fast. "I can ride fast, I can shoot, and I like adventure. Why not? I feel like my life is wasting away, herding cranky cattle all day and night."

Mr. Smart sighed and then smiled. "I wish there'd been something like this when I was young. Best of luck to you, Billy. Don't be a stranger around these parts though. You can send one of those letters up here once in a while to let me know how you're doing."

"Yes, sir. Hey, I have to get going. I've got some more of these papers to post around before I head out. I'll get Sage to you somehow."

ALTHOUGH BILLY'S EXCITEMENT had a powerful effect on her, Mayme couldn't help but feel envious. She'd had a strong desire to rush after him and beg to hear more. But with Billy being Billy, she refrained. She had no intention of inflating his ego even more than it was. Indeed all said, she couldn't help but feel a sort of self-loathing for being a girl. The flier had specifically required boys. Or had it?

Mayme read and re-read the flyer several times over the rest of the day. She had trouble focusing on anything else, frankly, and watched from a distance as several men and boys stopped to read it. She couldn't help the unkind thoughts she had about each of them. She silently urged them to quickly move on.

After Mr. Smart closed the mercantile for the day, she waited discretely in the shadows until he pointed Ox toward home. She checked to make sure no one was watching, and, when the coast was clear, pulled the paper off the door. As she quickly walked away, she folded it and shoved into her bodice. She had no idea what she was going to do with it. She just knew she had to take it down and keep it for her own. She needed to think. A sense of desperation awoke inside her and continued to grow as she walked home. She felt an intense desire to share this with someone. Yet she wasn't sure who would understand. But by the time she arrived home, she'd made a decision. She was somehow going to be one of those post riders.

MAYME PACED ALONGSIDE her bed, frequently glancing at the flyer lying on the folded blanket at the foot of it. The words were permanently emblazoned in her memory yet it seemed to constantly hail for her attention. The draw was too great for her not to read it again and again.

A post rider. What a dream come true it would be if she could pull it off. And it was something she was confident she could do. She was a fast rider. Images of her atop Blaze, racing through the fields sped through her mind. And thanks to Mr. Smart, she could now skillfully handle a gun. Although she wasn't too keen on the notion she might have to shoot somebody if the need arose. But if it were a matter of life or death, she didn't think she'd hesitate to pull the trigger.

The door flew open and Iris poked her head in. "You coming for dinner?"

Mayme followed Iris's eyes to the flyer. Her heart flew into her throat.

"Hey, what's that?" Iris swept into the room and grabbed the paper before Mayme could react.

"It's nothing. Give it here." She watched Iris's eyes moved across the page.

"Where'd you get this?"

"Billy Prescott brought it by today."

"So why do you have it? Isn't this something that should be posted on the door?" Iris's eyes suddenly grew large and her face fell slack. "You can't honestly think you could do something like this." She shook the flyer at Mayme. "It specifically says boys. In case you've forgotten, you're a girl."

"It says *fellows*, not boys." Mayme crossed her arms over her chest, defiantly defending her decision even though she hadn't exactly admitted her plans.

"Mayme, are you nuts? This ain't no job for a girl." Iris sat down on the bed and read the words again. She slumped slightly forward and bent her neck down.

"Isn't," Mayme corrected. She shook her head, realizing it sounded as if she was in agreement. "I know I can do it. Besides, I'm going to see if they'll give me a route from here down to the station in Pocatello. Billy said that was the safest anyway."

"Billy thinks you should do this?"

"No. No one knows but you."

"There's still the issue of you not being a boy."

"I'm going to cut my hair. You said yourself that when I have on my trousers and hat I look like a fellow."

Iris looked pointedly at Mayme's breasts. "What are you going to do about those?"

"God, I have no idea. I forgot about them. Maybe I can wrap them and wear loose shirts. I should be able to hide them. They're not that big."

"Yet."

"I'll figure something out."

Iris sighed loudly. "I just don't understand why you'd want to do something as crazy as this. Aren't you happy here? Don't you like us?"

Mayme sat beside Iris and put her arm around her shoulder. "Of course I do. Don't be silly. But I *know* I can do this. It'd be something I'd be really good at." She sighed. "Ever since my parents sent me away, I've felt inadequate.

Iris shook her head. "But you're not. You have a great job at the mercantile. Why can't you keep on doing that?"

All of a sudden, it became clear to Mayme. "Because I don't want to feel like I'm waiting around for some man to ask me to be his wife. I want to actually do something with my life that counts."

Iris stared at her for several moments, seemingly letting her words sink in. The corners of her mouth slowly turned up into a smile. "I'm the only one who knows?"

Mayme chuckled. "Yes. For the time being that is. But at some point I'm going to have to tell Mr. Smart. I can't just quit without saying anything."

"Do you think he'll hire me in your place?"

Mayme shoved her shoulder into Iris.' "You just want my job so you'll see Billy Prescott. Although I'm not sure how often you'll see him. He's already got one of these jobs."

Iris shrugged and laughed before becoming serious again. "You'll need someone to cut your hair. I can do that. And I'll help you with your clothes. There might even be something of my dad's still in the closet."

Mayme flung her arms around Iris and squeezed. "You're

the best. Thank you." The doubt and tension she felt about what she was about to attempt disappeared. In that single moment, Iris made her heart feel full. She wouldn't only be riding for the postal service. It'd be for Iris too.

IT TOOK A couple days for them to put together a collection of clothing for Mayme. Iris also found an old cloth wrap tucked deep in her father's closet. He'd used it to wrap his leg after pulling a groin muscle one time. After convincing Mayme it'd been washed, it was added to the pile. Mayme practiced wrapping her chest at night after everyone else went to bed. The last thing on the list of things to do would be to get her hair cut.

Mayme hadn't quite gathered the nerve to tell Mr. Smart about her plans. She was nervous and scared he'd either talk her out of it, or go to Mrs. Randall and blow the entire plot out of the water. She needed to think about it for a while longer.

In the meantime, with Iris's input, she practiced acting and speaking like a boy. By imitating what she remembered of Billy Prescott's behaviour, it was pretty easy. After her first few attempts brought about fits of muffled laughter and uncontrollable giggles, they were able to sober up enough to make progress.

"I think I should cut your hair before you go talk to Mr. Smart," Iris whispered to Mayme while washing dishes one evening.

Mayme was drying and sorting the cutlery. She paused and blinked at Iris as a fluttery feeling beat in her belly. "Why?"

"Let's put it this way. If you tell him looking and dressed like you do, you'll have a harder time convincing him you can do it. But if you walk into the mercantile and he doesn't recognize you—"

"He'd know I'm serious and be less likely try and talk me out of it." Mayme wasn't looking forward to having her lengthy tresses cut off. She'd had long hair for as long as she could remember.

"Oh, I suspect he'll still try to talk you out of it." Iris frowned and cocked her head. "But I'd be more willing to bet you'll feel more confident when you tell him you're quitting. And suggest I take your place." Iris' smile exuded mischief.

Mayme snorted and swatted her with the towel. "You're incorrigible." She leaned against the table and sighed. "You're probably right. Anyway, I should do it sooner rather than later so no one else gets the job."

"Mom will go over to Mrs. Cornelius' tomorrow night. I'll cut it after she leaves. But then you'll have to skip breakfast so Mom and the others don't see you. I'll make up some kind of excuse that you had to leave early for work."

"Okay. It's probably best your mom doesn't know . . . until I get the job anyway. I'll have to tell Mr. Smart I'll be late for work the next day. Otherwise he'll suspect something is up."

"Good idea."

"This is getting really complicated. I feel a little guilty for all the lying I'm having to do." She drew her shoulders up and tucked her elbows into her sides.

Not for the first time did she wish she were born a boy. She sure wouldn't have to go through all this trouble to get a job as a Post Rider. Then again, if she were a boy, her father would've taken her under his wing like she'd seen so many other fathers do. Boys were given a slap on the wrist and an excuse that they were learning about life. So in hindsight, she reasoned, were she the opposite sex, she'd never have this opportunity.

Chapter Eleven

MAYME FELT A slight tug as Iris lifted the first tuft of her hair.

"Last chance," Iris said.

The sheer blades squeaked against each other as she opened and closed them.

Mayme drew a deep breath, swallowed hard, and nodded.

"There's no going back after I cut it you know."

"Just do it and get it over with." Mayme jiggled her knee up and down.

The blades made a gritty sound as Iris made the first cut.

Snip. Squeak. Snip. Squeak. Snip.

Mayme closed her eyes and crinkled her nose. She felt the lock of soft hair hit the tightly clasped hands in her lap. After a few minutes she got brave enough to open her eyes. A small pile of hair had accumulated on her lap. She shook her hands and swiped it onto the floor. She looked down and realized how light her head felt with each snip of the sheers.

"Boy, you have a lot of hair. I could make a pillow out of it." Iris giggled.

"How do I look?"

"I'll let you know after I'm done. Right now you look like something the dog dragged in and then the rats made a nest in."

"Gee, thanks."

"Don't worry. When I'm finished, you won't recognize yourself."

"With a description like that, I'm sure not." Mayme ventured running a hand through the hair she had left. She was shocked to feel how short it was. But at the same time, she had to admit it kind of felt good. "Can I see?" She looked around for the hand-held mirror Iris had taken from her mother's room.

"Not yet. Give me a few more minutes."

Snip. Squeak. Snip. Squeak. Snip.

"Okay. Close your eyes," Iris said after a while.

Mayme did as told. She abruptly felt the handle of the mirror touch her palm. She hesitantly grasped it. She slid her right eye open and then the left, wavering between curiosity of what she looked like, and procrastination of how badly she might appear.

The boy who stared back at her in the mirror looked vaguely familiar. His eyes and nose looked like hers. But that was where the similarity stopped. His hair was understandably short and youthfully wavy. Her revelation came as she realized she nearly didn't recognize herself. She ran her hand back and forth over her scalp, enjoying the cool sensation.

Iris walked around in front of her and stared open-mouthed. "Forget, Billy. Wow. You're a handsome lad, Mayme."

"Oh my God. That's the one thing I haven't thought about. My name. I can hardly go by Mayme."

Iris chuckled. "No. No you can't." She grabbed her chin between her thumb and index finger. "Hmm. How about Nathaniel?"

"That's a bit long, don't you think?"

"You could go by Nathan, or Nate for short."

Mayme looked at her thoughtfully. "Where'd you come up with that?"

Iris clasped her hands in front of her mouth. "It was my dad's name. My mom used to call him Nathan, but most people called him Nate."

Mayme stood up and wrapped her arms around Iris. "I'd be honored to be known as Nathan. Thank you."

She could tell by the smile on Iris's face that she'd just cemented their future as lifelong friends.

MAYME'S EYES FLEW open in the middle of the night. The room was dark but for the stream of moonlight that beamed down onto the floor. *I need a horse. And a gun.*

She was already familiar with the cost of a carbine from the mercantile. From what she'd earned so far, she could almost afford it. *But a horse. How in heavens can I pay for a horse?* Suddenly she remembered the money Betty had given her the last night on the train. She threw the covers back and slid out of bed. She lit the oil lamp and lowered the wick. Annie sometimes got up in the middle of the night and she didn't need her seeing the light beneath the door and then knocking.

She pulled the bottom drawer of the dresser open and reached deep into the back, beneath the dress she'd arrived in. The money was still wrapped in a kerchief just like it was when she'd stowed it. She had never counted it, thinking it too rude. And besides, she'd had all intentions of returning it to Betty once she figured out how to get it to her.

She held the small wad closer to the light, unwrapped it, and began to count. With each flip of a note, her eyes grew wider. *Two hundred dollars?* "Where did Betty get all this money?" She shook her head in disbelief when she recalled what Betty had given her was just a small portion of the roll she had. "Ho-lee cow." She looked up and stared at the darkness. She had more than enough money for a rifle, horse, saddle and bridle, bedroll and possibly some extra clothing befitting a boy.

She heard a creak of the floor outside her door. She tucked the money back into the drawer, extinguished the lamp, and crept quietly back into bed. After her mind ceased racing with possibilities, she drifted off to a dream-filled sleep.

A QUIET KNOCK on her door woke her before sunup. Iris stuck her head in. The lamp she held cast a stream of yellow light onto Mayme's dresser.

"You'd best get up and get going," Iris whispered. She set a thick slice of bread onto the dresser. "This should hold you over for a while. Good luck."

"Thank you." Mayme's mouth watered at the sight. The bread was smeared with butter and blueberry preserves.

Iris soundlessly closed the door, leaving Mayme to alternately dress and take bites of the bread. Last night, knowing she'd have to hurry in the morning, she'd laid out the chest wrap, underwear, trousers, and the flannel shirt Iris had given her.

She'd finished dressing and looked down at her feet. Fortunately the trousers were long enough to cover the shoes she'd don when she got outside. She mentally added chaps and a pair of boots to the list of necessities to buy. She checked her reflection in the mirror and mussed her hair up a bit more. Satisfied, she finished off the last bite of bread, picked up her shoes, and opened the door. She was convinced the pounding of her heart would awaken the rest of the house as she descended the stairs. She slipped out the front door and sat outside on the porch, finally able to take a breath. So far so good.

The first orange hued rays of sunrise kissed the tops of the mountains and reflected off the already dust laden air. A robin serenaded the morning with its *cheerio-cheeriup* song from a tree near the church. Mayme barely noticed the cool breeze.

She took her time walking down the road. It was difficult to avoid falling in the ruts while concentrating on walking like a boy. Her heart nearly leapt into her throat as Mr. Smart passed by in the wagon. Ox flicked his ears back and forth and his nostrils flared as he went by. Mayme was convinced she didn't fool the horse. He knew exactly who she was.

The routine of opening the mercantile never changed. She knew Mr. Smart would be moving tools out onto the porch just as she did every morning. She still felt guilty for feeding him the little white lie about having to go to the doctor for women's reasons. But she thought he'd understand when she finally revealed herself to him.

If Ox hadn't nickered to her as she rounded the back of the building, she would've stridden right in without a thought. She quickly realized her error and turned on her heal in the direction of the front.

She took a minute to gather her nerve. She slowed her

breathing and practiced deepening her voice a bit. *It's now or never.*

Unbelievably Mr. Smart was already waiting on a customer. He glanced up and nodded to acknowledge her as she walked through the door. He'd taught her early on that if a customer knew they'd been seen, they'd be less likely to walk out before they were tended to.

She nonchalantly walked to the counter and with renewed interest, examined the guns. Which one should she buy? The obvious choice was the Winchester Mr. Smart taught her to shoot with. Not only did she know the ins-and-out of it, she was comfortable handling it.

The bell on the cash register rang, signalling the end of the transaction with the other customer.

"What can I get for you?" Mr. Smart moved closer but didn't obstruct her view of the guns.

"I, uh—" She nearly panicked but held fast. She took a deep breath, swallowed the lump in her throat, and said the first thing she could think of. "I need a box of SSA's."

"SSA's?"

Realizing her mistake, she cleared her throat and quickly corrected herself. "I mean SAA's."

Mr. Smart cocked his head and narrowed his eyes. "What kind of gun do you have, son?"

She cast her eyes down and tried to remember what kind of gun Billy carried. *Oh no. Those bullets are for pistols and I know nothing about them!*

Mayme laughed nervously. "I mean I need some bullets for my rifle. It's, um, a Winchester lever action. I guess I need those kind."

"Right." He made no move to retrieve the bullets from the drawer. "I don't think I've ever seen you around in these parts. Hey, I do remember."

Mayme nearly wet herself.

"That was you on the road earlier, wasn't it?"

She nodded.

"I figure a fella dressed like you should be riding. You do

have a horse, don't you, son?" Mr. Smart crossed his arms over his chest and stood directly in front of her.

Mayme could feel his scrutinizing gaze drift over her.

"I'm going to be buying one soon."

"When? After your doctor's appointment? What the heck are you up to, Mayme?"

Mayme's mouth fell open. She stared at him incredulously. She finally found her voice. But it was Mayme Watson's voice, not Nathan—She realized another mistake. They hadn't come up with a last name for her.

"Mayme?"

She slapped her hips and stomped a foot. "Gosh darn it. You weren't supposed to recognize me."

"May I ask why?"

There was no point in lying anymore. She needed Mr. Smart's help. She had to come clean and tell him the truth.

"Because I'm going to get a job as a post rider. Just like Billy."

Mr. Smart snorted. "You can't be serious. Besides, the flyer specifically said they only wanted boys."

Mayme watched as realization crossed Mr. Smart's face.

"I could do that job. I'm an excellent rider. And a good shot. You said that yourself."

Mr. Smart turned abruptly and disappeared into to the back room.

Mayme gawked open-mouthed for a moment and then followed. She found him staring at the photo of his wife.

"Mr. Smart?"

He didn't answer.

"I'm sorry for lying to you. I just really want this job and since you know me, I thought I should test my disguise on you." She sighed. "But it obviously didn't work. I don't know who I was trying to fool more. Probably me." She realized she was babbling and closed her mouth.

It seems like hours passed before Mr. Smart said anything, although the first sound from him was a heavy sigh. He smoothed the sides of his moustache down around his mouth in long strokes.

"If I were your father, I'd probably ground you for even thinking about such a ludicrous thing, let alone attempting it."

"But—"

He raised a finger up. "Let me finish."

Mayme slouched down on a stool used to get thing off high shelves. She dropped her chin to her chest and folded her arms against her middle. Her posture mirrored that of the girl in Chicago who'd been lectured to for hours by an enraged father and an inebriated mother. Her cheeks burned with embarrassment. How did she ever think she could get away with something so preposterous? She would give up any notions and do exactly what Mrs. Randall had suggested: bide her time for a husband. Her stomach churned with the idea. She'd rather crawl into a hole, shrivel up and move on to the next life.

"I've told you before how I wished my daughter had known how to shoot. Lord knows I pushed her to learn everything else: gentle a horse to ride, build a fire, cut firewood. I wanted her to be as self-sufficient as possible. She was just taken from me too soon." He took the photo off the nail and slid his back down the wall so he sat directly across from Mayme. "I've come to think of you as a daughter, Mayme. Which puts me in a difficult predicament. My first inclination is to absolutely forbid you to carry on with this idea. But I don't have that right, now do I?"

Mayme raised her head and studied him. He looked more serious than she'd ever seen him. He spoke carefully and seemed to choose his words meticulously. She thought he might be doing his best to understand and at the same time, reason with himself. The difference between her father and Mr. Smart was the fact that the later did not appear angry.

"Before we had children, my wife and I agreed we'd never hold them too close. Whether we had boys or girls, we wanted them to build a life, not just live it. Do you understand what I mean?"

Mayme shook her head.

"When you're growing up, you tend to get told that the

world is the way it is and you can't change it. Your purpose is to live your life inside of that world. Try not to get into too much trouble, go to school, get married and have kids. But life can be a lot broader than that if you realize one simple thing. You can build your own life that others can live in too."

"I don't understand what that has to do with what I want to do."

Mr. Smart got to his feet and returned the photo to its place on the wall. "Mayme, I'm trying to tell you that, although I'll worry myself sick about you, I won't hold you back. Instead, I'll help you with whatever you need. Since you came here, you've helped me to step out of my grief. I too am learning something new about life."

Mayme jumped up and before she could think, threw her arms around him. A moment later, Mr. Smart hugged her in return.

"Thank you." She fought the tears at first and then gave in to them.

"Promise me one thing."

Mayme stepped back, sniffed, wiped her eyes, and nodded.

"You be damned careful out there. And if you need a place to stay when you're in the area, I have an extra room. You'll always be welcome."

"I will. I promise."

"Come with me." Mr. Smart walked out and stopped behind the counter next to the guns. He unlocked the security chain and removed the Winchester. "You'll need a firearm." He opened the ammunition drawer and took out two one-hundred-count boxes of bullets. "At least now when you apply for the job, you'll look the part."

"That's the one I was going to buy. I'll bring the money in tomorrow." Mayme took the rifle and then shoved the bullets in the pockets of her trousers and flannel shirt.

"Nope. I won't hear of it. Consider it a gift from a good friend. If you get the job, we'll talk about what else you'll need."

Mayme knew better than to refuse. It'd be useless. Instead she said, "I wish you *were* my father."

This time Mr. Smart had a tear in his eye. "Go on now. Tomorrow morning I want to hear you got that job."

Mayme smiled. "Yes, sir."

Chapter Twelve

SHE WALKED THE length of town and then some to get to the post office. It was housed in a white-washed shack close to the railroad station. She cussed silently as she navigated the rutted road. Weighted down by the rifle and what felt like ten pounds of bullets, trickles of sweat seeped from her chest wrap. By the time she arrived, her shirt had plastered itself to her skin. Except over her covered breasts. She pulled the material away and flapped it to dry as best she could. There were a few people waiting in line, so she took the opportunity to splash some water on her face from a water trough used primarily by the stagecoach horses. By the time she dried her face and brushed the dust off her clothes, the post office was free of customers.

Feeling refreshed and more confident, she took a bold hop onto the porch and walked in.

The man looked up and her heart skipped a beat. He was the very same man who ran the ticket counter for the train. She hid her surprise and strode up to the counter. So far she saw no recognition on his face.

Counter to ceiling iron bars completed the cage in which the man sat. A wooden structure with a series of square compartments lined the back wall. Several were filled with envelopes and assorted scrolls. To the right was a framed Postmaster certificate. She assumed he was the named Lawrence Heyburn noted.

"May I help you?" Lawrence peered over the top of his glasses.

"Yes, sir. I'm here to apply for a post rider job." Mayme rested the gun in the crook of her arm.

"Can you ride fast?"

"Yes, sir." Mayme thanked her lucky stars he didn't ask if she had a horse.

"Can you shoot?"

"Yes, sir. Exceptionally, if I do say so myself." Mayme kept her eyes locked on his.

"Very well." Lawrence rose from his seat and retrieved a scroll from behind him. He unrolled what she now recognized as a crudely sketched map. Several notes with names had been written along lines drawn in all directions. He studied the map in silence, rubbing the stubble on his pointy chin. "Most of the routes have been filled."

Mayme's heart sank as she stared wordlessly at the map.

"However," he said, running his finger over the parchment. "There's a route to Oro Fino Creek that needs a rider. A man named Pierce discovered gold up there and now there's enough settlers up there for a mail delivery."

"I'll take it," Mayme said quickly.

Lawrence inspected her over his spectacles. "Hold on there, son. This here route runs through some pretty rough country." Mayme just kept her steady gaze on him. "And it's a year round job you know. Snow gets deep up there. It may be more of a job for a man."

Mayme shrugged and said in a firm voice, "I can handle it. When can I start?"

Lawrence acknowledged her acceptance by sliding a piece of paper and pencil in her direction. "Do you know how to read and write?"

"Yes, sir."

"Good. Then write your name and who to contact in case something happens to you."

Mayme had excelled in and was quite proud of her penmanship. However she knew she had to tone it down quite a bit so it wouldn't look so feminine. So she chose to use rudimentary letters instead of cursive. On a whim she used Adams as her last name. It didn't take much thought to write Mr. Smart down as her contact.

Lawrence nodded as she returned the paper and pencil.

"Very good." He handed her another paper. "Raise your

right hand and read this aloud. It's an oath to hold you to your responsibilities."

Mayme picked it up, raised her right hand, and began. "I, Nathan Adams, do hereby swear before the Great and Living God, that while I am an employee of the United States Post, I will under no circumstances use profane language, that I will refrain from consuming any intoxicating drinks, that I will not quarrel or fight with any other employee of the United States Post, and that in every respect, I will conduct myself honestly, be faithful to my duties, and so direct all my acts as to win the confidence of my employer, so help me God."

"So help you, God," he repeated. "Excellent. Now come back tomorrow. I'll give you a map of your route. If you're lucky you'll be riding by next week."

Mayme's heart beat fast. A lightness spread through her chest as reality took hold. "Yes, sir. Thank you, sir." She turned on her heel and barely managed to walk out without a yell of triumph, although her walk became a fast-paced strut once her feet hit the dirt.

She couldn't wait to tell Iris and Mr. Smart. Then she remembered there were a few other people who might not be as excited when she shared the news.

THE CLOSER SHE got to home, the less eager she became in regards to facing Mrs. Randall. She wondered if Iris had mentioned anything to her. In a way she wouldn't have at all minded. Then she might not have had to deal Mrs. Randall's imminent disapproval. But no, she decided, she'd have to be mature enough to face her on her own.

The house was quiet as she walked through the front door. This came as no surprise as it was only mid-afternoon. She peeked into the parlor on her way past, but the room was vacant.

Quiet voices came down the hall from the kitchen. The delectable smell of a roast wafted throughout. Her mouth watered and her stomach clenched in hunger. Until now her nerves and excitement had dampened her appetite.

She walked through the kitchen entrance, and Mrs. Randall stopped speaking in mid-sentence. Annie's giggle came to an abrupt halt and the smile melted from her face. They both openly stared at her with their mouths hanging open.

"You'll catch flies like that," Mayme jokingly said with Nathan's voice.

Mrs. Randall gaped once and swallowed hard. "Annie, leave us."

Annie remained frozen to the spot, holding a spoon over a pot of peeled potatoes.

"Annie. At once."

Mrs. Randall's voice was steely enough to motivate Annie to spring into action. She dropped the spoon and continued to stare at Mayme as she sidestepped to the door. She took one last look at her before fleeing down the hall. Mayme guessed she'd spend the next hour or so searching in vain for a housemate to tell. She felt safe in knowing Annie didn't know anyone outside the home. Iris would make sure her secret stayed within the walls of the house.

If not for the cold expression on Mrs. Randall's face, Mayme would've thought the situation comical. But sadly, it was anything but.

"Would you like to explain yourself, young lady?"

"Yes, ma'am. I got a job as a post rider for the postal service. But I had to disguise myself as a boy in order to get it."

Mrs. Randall clamped her jaw. "I see," she said through set teeth. She cleared her throat, pulled a chair out from the table and sat down. "First of all, do you realize how ridiculous you look? Honestly, Mayme, you look like an unschooled ranch hand. What have you done to your beautiful hair?"

"Iris cut—"

"You involved my daughter in this mockery? I thought I made myself clear that you were to act like a sensible young woman. You're a disgrace, Miss Watson. I cannot allow you to set such a hideous example for the other girls, most of all Iris. I most definitely do not want her getting ideas in her head that reflect anything equally as absurd and outrageous."

For just an instant, Mayme felt herself folding under the stern discipline. It was an ingrained habit and she couldn't help herself, but something deep within her rebelled. It was *her* life, *her* decision. Gone were the days when she was forced to seek approval from an adult or maintain an air of wealth and act like a lady.

"I appreciate your concern. Maybe if I were Iris's mother, I'd share the same apprehension. But in the end I would hope I'd encourage my daughter to be who and what she wants and not try to hold her back."

Mrs. Randall's eyes bored into her own. Her continued agitation was evident by the constant drumming of her fingers on the table.

"I'm going to ride and deliver mail. I've already taken the oath and signed the papers."

"I obviously can't stop you. It's plain you're too hard headed to see any reason. But I will not allow you, under any circumstances to have contact with the other girls."

"Are you kicking me out?" Mayme's mind raced as a strand of uncertainty tried to take hold.

"I wouldn't be held as so cruel. You will take your meals separately. You will leave this house in the morning before anyone rises and upon your return stay confined to your room until the others retire. I will make sure an evening meal is set outside your door. Have I made myself clear?"

"Yes, ma'am." Mayme silently prayed she'd be in the saddle sooner than what she'd been told. She wasn't sure she'd be able to cope living under the prison-like conditions Mrs Randall was enforcing.

LATER THAT EVENING, as Mayme lay in bed, she fought to not feel sorry for herself. It was difficult not being able to share her news with the others. And she missed Iris. They'd grown closer while conspiring. Iris was the sister she'd never had.

A light scratching preceded the door opening a crack.

"Are you awake?" Iris said in quiet whisper.

"Yes." Mayme sat up and straightened her covers.

Iris disappeared for a moment and then slipped through the door. She gave Mayme a devilish smile and joined her on bed.

"You shouldn't be in here. What if your mom catches you?"

"It'll be okay. She's asleep. I saw her sneak some whiskey into her tea tonight after she told us we were supposed to stay away from you for a while. She said you had some contagious disease and we weren't supposed to tell anyone. Annie had a stupid grin on her face the whole night."

Mayme shook her head. "I'm sure she did. She was in the kitchen with your mom when I came home, so she knows what I look like." She gasped. "I can't believe your mom lied outright like that."

"I know. She's a proud woman and sometimes it gets the better of her." Iris bounced up and down and her eyes got big. "Tell me. Did Mr. Smart recognize you? And oh! You got the job, right?"

"Yeah, he recognized me all right. He wasn't happy at first, but it all turned out okay. Getting the route was pretty easy, actually. The man bought my act, hook, line, and sinker."

"When do you start?" Iris' excitement was contagious.

Mayme leaned forward and grasped Iris' arm. "Hopefully next week. But I have a lot to do before then. I need to get a horse and saddle and stuff."

"I guess it's just your luck that a herd of horses came into the sale lot this afternoon. I don't know a lot about horses, but there sure are some pretty ones there."

Mayme chuckled. "Pretty doesn't get you far if they don't have good legs. I'll see if Mr. Smart will come with me to have a look at them tomorrow."

"I have to go, in case Mom gets up to use the outhouse. I'll come back tomorrow night."

"Okay. Be careful." Mayme gave Iris a quick hug and then she was gone.

Iris's visit had instilled some joy in an otherwise bleak evening. And tomorrow she might be buying a horse. *I sure hope there's some good ones there.*

Chapter Thirteen

MAYME AND MR. Smart rested their arms across the top railing of the holding pen. The forty horses stood lazily in the early morning sun. Their heads dripped low. A couple swished their tails in agitation as a bay yearling colt trotted by and faked a buck as he passed. His eyes were alert and had a mischievous gleam in them.

"He looks like he'd be a handful," Mayme said.

"My guess is he's not gelded yet." Mr. Smart shoved his hat farther down on his head to block the sun on his face.

A wagon on which a pile of hay sat precariously, rattled up alongside the fence. It was pulled by a flea-bitten grey. Mayme assumed this was a normal job as he ignored the horses in the paddock. Armed with a pitchfork, the man speared the hay and threw it over the fence in separate piles. The horses hurried in a sudden surge to get their share.

"Hi, Fred. Looking for some new blood to put in your herd?"

"Good morning, Tom. I'm not, but my friend here is. Sh-He'll be riding for the post, so we're looking for a horse that's hardy and can do the miles."

"Ah, right. Well, there's a couple of them in there that might meet his needs. That black one with the white blaze is nice. My first pick would be the chestnut with the four white socks, but it looks like she bowed a tendon sometime in the past."

"What about that blue roan?" Mayme climbed higher onto the fence and pointed. "She looks solid as they come." She looked down at Mr. Smart. "Can we go look at her?"

"Hey, Tom. You mind if we check out that roan in there?"

"Have at it. She's a nice one and broke good. I don't know if she's been bred or not. My guess is no. I think that's the one

Madison said wouldn't let the stud near her. So she was no good to him."

Mayme climbed over the fence and dropped to the ground before the man had finished talking.

The mare seemed to notice Mayme's approach immediately. Strands of hay hung out both sides of her mouth. She chewed methodically and flared her nostrils to gain Mayme's scent.

The horse remained alert but calm as Mayme came to stand at her side. Her ears twitched forward and the one on the nearest side twisted toward her. Mayme put her hand on the muscled neck. The mare didn't flinch other than to bring her head lower and watch Mayme with a kind liquid-brown eye. Mayme knew this as a good sign.

She stood back and assessed the mare's condition. Her ribs were covered with a thin layer of fat, but were visible when she took a deep breath. Her nicely shaped neck blended into strong shoulders, which led to a short back and toward powerful haunches.

Her conformation was correct. So much so that Mayme knew she'd be a comfortable ride. She ran her hands down the mare's legs. Everything seemed perfect. Until she came to her feet. All four striped hooves were overgrown and ragged around the edges.

"Looks like she has some Appaloosa in her." Mr Smart crouched down beside Mayme. "Those cracks are only cosmetic. If you end up buying her, we'll get some shoes put on her and she'll be fine. Appaloosas have notoriously good feet. Having been in a big herd, these just haven't been cared for properly."

The mare sniffed Mayme's neck and nudged her gently.

"I think she's taken a liking to you." Mr. Smart stood up and ran his hands over her back. "She's strong. A good brushing would do her good." He lifted the mare's top lip and examined her teeth. "She looks to be about five or six years old. Heck, May-Nathan, if you don't buy her, I will."

Mayme got up and went to the horse's head. She stroked the mare's face from her forehead down to her jowls. There was something maternal about this horse. When she looked into the mare's eyes and saw brown softness she made her mind up. She wanted her.

"How much do you suppose she is?"

"No idea. I'll go ask Tom and see what they're asking." He patted her on the shoulder. "I don't think I'd worry much about you on the trail aboard this one. I'll be back in a minute."

Neither Mayme nor the mare paid any attention as Mr. Smart walked away.

"Hey, big girl. What do you think? Want to run through the mountains with me?" Mayme blew softly into her nostrils and was pleased when the mare rubbed her upper lip against her cheek.

Mr. Smart rubbed the back of his neck as he walked back a few minutes later.

"Uh oh. You don't look like you have good news for me." Mayme pressed her lips tightly and frowned. A feeling of dread overcame her. She took a deep breath and waited for the disappointment.

"Can you afford twenty dollars?" Mr. Smart squinted painfully.

"That's all she's going to cost?"

"Well, Tom said they were looking to get a hundred for her. But he said if I threw in a breeding to Cloud, you could have her for twenty."

Mayme's eyes misted. "So she's nearly mine?"

"Yep. You just have to hand over the twenty note. There is one problem though."

Mayme scanned the horse, wondering what could possibly be wrong with her. She looked at Mr. Smart with raised eyebrows.

"You don't have a name for her yet."

Mayme blew out a breath and rubbed her cheek. "Geez. You scared me. But you're right." She took two steps back and scanned the mare's hide. Her roaning pattern was unlike anything she'd ever seen. Her black-based coat was dusted with little flecks of white. The mingling of the white and black caused a blue sheen to cover her body. Her head and lower legs were black which complemented the silver of her mane and tail.

Mayme smiled and nodded. "Her name is Duster," she said proudly.

THEY TOOK DUSTER to the livery and arranged to have shoes put on, and rented a stall for her. Mr. Smart had offered to take Duster to his farm, but Mayme wanted her close by so they could get to know each other. She cringed at paying the fifty cents per day, but she knew it was only temporary.

Mayme purchased a saddle and bridle at the livery as well. She didn't want to leave her newly acquired tack at the stable, nor could she take them home. So she accepted Mr. Smart's offer to keep it in the back room at the mercantile. That way they wouldn't be so difficult to carry the short distance to the livery, and it would give her the opportunity to give them a good oiling before she hit the trail.

She left Mr. Smart to run the store. She felt bad that he might have lost some business due to opening late, but she was pleased he'd been with her that morning. If not for the adventures that lie ahead of her, she might've been sadder at not working alongside Mr. Smart.

Like the day before, she had to allow the postmaster to finish waiting on people wishing to send telegraphs or conduct other business. She sat on the step outside and watched the wind build mini twisters with the dust.

"You may come in now, Mr. Adams."

It took Mayme a second to realize that he was calling for her.

She scrambled to her feet and trotted inside.

"Hello, sir."

Lawrence nodded and smiled at her briefly. "Since you've returned, I'm guessing you still wish to honor the position."

"Yes, sir. I thought it was a sure thing when I took the oath."

"Well, lad, you'd be surprised how many fellows come in and do just that. Then they never show up again because their mothers have talked them out of it or they decide they're not brave enough."

Lawrence rummaged under the counter and pulled out what looked like a saddlebag with extra leather.

"This is your mochila." He held it up. "It's specially designed to carry mail. The hole in the front fits over the saddle horn and the slit fits over the cantle behind you. These boxes, the cantines stay locked at all times as this is where the mail is kept."

Mayme took the mochila from Lawrence and looked at the small leather boxes. Each was already locked.

"Is there mail in here already?"

"Oddly, yes. Some letters were diverted from yesterday's train. I've already sent off a telegraph to Oro Fino Creek and they'll be expecting you by the end of next week." Lawrence handed her a folded parchment. "This is the map to guide you there. Mind you, there is no specific route as of yet. The majority of trails that lead into Oro Fino come from the east, so you'll have to find your way."

"Okay." Mayme felt a moment of indecision. She ran her hands down the front of her trousers. "Well . . ."

"Are you having second thoughts?" Lawrence narrowed his eyes at her.

She inhaled deeply through her nose and exhaled through her mouth. *This is what I wanted, what my heart called for. I can do this. And besides, I won't be alone. I have Duster . . . and my guns.*

"What I was about to say was, well, I'd best get going then."

"Very well. May God guide you safely on your travels."

Mayme headed for the livery. Her step became livelier as she reminded herself she had a horse. And a job that required her to be on said horse.

Duster's deep nicker welcomed her as she walked into the barn. None of the bedding in stall had been disturbed and Mayme wondered if Duster had stood at the stall door awaiting her return. She peeked over the stall and was satisfied to see that the farrier had already trimmed and put shoes on Duster's hooves. They looked as good as Blaze's did after he was shod.

"Hey, big girl. What do you say we get to know each other? We're going to be heading out on a long trail ride in a few days." Mayme stroked Duster's neck and her hand came away with a bunch of hair pasted on it. She looked around and smiled as she found a burlap sack that'd been emptied of the oats once stored in it. She took it outside and flapped the dust out of it. Satisfied, she went into Duster's stall and let her sniff it before she touched her with it.

Duster snorted twice and wiggled her nose over the sack.

"Still smell the oats, huh girl." Mayme rubbed the sack gently on Duster's chest.

Duster's nose wiggled back and forth, and Mayme used a bit more force. Pretty soon she was able to work the burlap over Duster's entire hide. Mayme was hot and sweaty by the time she finished and believed she wore more hair and dirt on her than Duster did. She wiped her face with a sleeve. And pasted her hair back under her hat.

As during her grooming, Duster stood stock still as Mayme laid the saddle on her back. Mayme tightened the girth and Duster didn't move. Mayme held the bridle in front of Duster's face, and she lowered her head, opened her mouth, and took the bit without any drama whatsoever.

"Wow. You really have nice ground manners. But let's see how you ride, shall we?"

Mayme led Duster out of the barn. After she adjusted the stirrups to her length, she stepped up and swung her leg over Duster's back. She wiggled her butt back and forth in the saddle to set it firmly on Dusters back. She picked up the reins and patted Duster's neck.

"Okay, big girl. Let's see what you can do."

Mayme quickly realized Duster reacted to weight adjustment in the stirrups more than signals with her legs or reins, although she was keen to do those as well.

She followed the road out of town, past the train station.

The ruts ran out and turned into a dusty trail, and she eased Duster into a trot. As she suspected, Duster's stride was easy and extremely comfortable. She asked for a canter, and Duster cross-cantered a few strides before correcting herself.

Mayme was impressed with Duster's endurance. She'd barely broken a sweat until after she'd slowed her down to catch her breath. "It's *me* that's not used to riding."

Already her legs were tired and the rocker bones in her seat were letting her know of their presence. She decided to turn around and head back. There'd be plenty of time for her to get used to the long hours in the saddle.

"YOU'LL NEED THIS." A long chain with a pocket watch attached at the end dangled from Mr. Smart's fingers. "It's as important as the flint."

Mayme gazed at the watch. "I can tell pretty good time from the position of the sun."

"I'm sure you can. But this is also your compass."

"What?"

"Follow me." Mr. Smart led the way out the back of the store. He looked up at the sky and moved out of the shadow of the building. "You'll use this to check your course. If you divide the watch into three-hundred sixty degrees, or like the points on a compass, you can figure out a line of direction from north to south."

"How the heck do I do that?"

He held the watch in front of him. "You aim the hour hand at the sun. Then you split the distance between the hour hand and the twelve on the watch. See? It's eight-fifteen in the morning now. The split is near ten which shows you the southern direction and north is where the four is."

Mayme furrowed her brows in concentration.

"Look, you have any doubt which end of the line is north, just remember that the sun rises in the east, sets in the west, and is due south at noon."

"The sun is in the east before noon and in the west after noon." Mayme nodded. "Okay. I understand."

"There's one other thing you have to remember." Mr. Smart handed the watch to her. "You have to keep it wound. An hour difference could take you in a completely wrong direction. You surely don't want to get lost in those mountains."

Mayme focused on the mountains in the distance. Suddenly they looked less pretty and more foreboding.

"YOU'RE LEAVING IN only two days?" Iris said that night. "That's not near long enough for me to get used to you leaving."

Mayme smiled at her and patted her hand. "I'd leave tomorrow except I have to buy provisions, a bedroll, and a few other things that I didn't have time to get today. I would've liked to take Duster on some longer rides too. I rode her out past the train station and back today. I was so proud of her. She was so steady and didn't even spook when I had to shoot the rattlesnake."

Iris shook her head and chuckled. "You are nothing like the girl who came off that train a few months back."

"I am. I'm just not adhering to everybody else's thoughts of how a girl should look and act." Mayme winked at her. "I guess I did go from one extreme to the other."

MAYME WAS ABLE to purchase most of what she needed from Mr. Smart. He didn't want to take her money at first, but after she nearly cleaned him out of dried meat, biscuits, and bullets, he relented. But only after he added a flint and knife to her pile.

She stood back and surveyed her purchases. "Geez. I don't know how I'm going to carry all this."

"Roll your clothes up inside your bedroll. You should be able to pack the rest into the saddlebags. Keep your flint inside your pocket because you never know when you'll need to make a fast fire or a torch. And one last, but very important thing: *Always* keep your guns loaded."

"Yes, sir."

"Good. I'll see you when you get back." Mr. Smart wrapped his arms around her and squeezed. "You be careful out there and hurry home, you hear?"

MAYME ROSE BEFORE dawn the next morning. There wasn't anything else of hers in the room except the clothes she would wear. She had packed her suitcase with everything she wouldn't need. It was now safely stored in Iris's room. She wrapped her chest, shoved her arms through the flannel shirt, and tied a bandanna around her neck. Once she'd pulled on her trousers, she tucked her shirt inside the hem and threaded an ammunition belt through the loops. Although it held twenty-four rounds, it wasn't obtrusive sitting on her hips. After sliding her feet into her new boots, she took one last look around her room. It looked as if she'd never been there.

She took a deep breath and let it out slowly. "Time to go." Thankfully everyone else was still asleep in her respective rooms. As she crept downstairs, she placed her palm on Iris's door. "I'll miss you most of all."

Chapter Fourteen

DUSTER DANCED IN place as if she knew they were about to embark on a big adventure. She tossed her head proudly and snorted.

"Easy girl. You don't want to wear yourself out before we get out of town." Mayme patted Duster's neck. She circled the horse, making sure everything was securely tied, and then checked it again.

"Thank heavens I caught you before you left," Mayme heard Iris say as she finished tightening the girth.

She freed the hooked stirrup from the horn, let it down, and turned around.

Iris shoved a small sack into Mayme's hands. "I made these for you."

Mayme opened the sack to find a several pieces of fried bread, each with a hole in it. She looked at Iris with raised eyebrows.

"I put holes in them so you could just poke a finger in and eat them as you rode."

"Oh! What a great idea. Thank you." Mayme realized that she now had to say goodbye to Iris again. She felt a lump working its way into her throat and suddenly she couldn't find her voice, couldn't find the words to tell Iris what her friendship meant to her.

Iris must have read the look on Mayme's face. She pulled her into a hug and then pushed her toward Duster. "You better get going. I'll see you when I see you."

Mayme smiled weakly and tied the sack onto the saddle horn. She stepped into the stirrup and pulled herself up into the saddle. She tipped her hat and said, "Yeah. Count on it."

She pushed Duster into a slow trot to expel any lingering thoughts of changing her mind and staying. By the time she reached the town's western edge, her concentration was solely focused on moving in rhythm with Duster's gaits. Not for the first time, she gloried in being on the back of a horse again. She'd missed the wind in her hair, the smell of horse sweat, and the creak of leather. Duster felt good beneath her and didn't seem to be bothered by the weight of all her gear.

The sun was high in the sky before she finally reached the point where she had to change direction and head north. The land fell away in gullies and ravines to the river. According to the map, she had to cross here.

Mayme pulled Duster up and double-checked the map. From her vantage point, she saw steep rolling hills that led up to huge outcroppings of underlying granite and gaunt pines that towered somberly everywhere. It all seemed so wild and untamed to her mid-west bred eyes.

A barely perceptible cattle trail led her eyes to the river below. Beyond, the trail cut through a wall of white birch trees. She clucked to Duster, leaned back in the saddle, and let Duster pick her way down the rocky slope littered with rocks and old piles of cattle dung.

The closer she got to the river, the wider it seemed to grow. Large boulders were spattered downstream just before a series of rapids rippled the water. Mayme scanned the current for the best place to cross and found a spot where it seemed calmer. She pointed Duster toward the river and entered the water. The sloshing and dull thuds of hooves meeting the rocks beneath the water mixed with the breeze created by the river.

Aside from a few stumbles, which Duster easily recovered from, the crossing was uneventful. Convinced they both could use a break, Mayme dismounted on the other side. While Duster drank her fill from the river edge, Mayme sipped from her canteen. As she did so, she scanned Duster's legs and made sure the shoes were still securely nailed to her hooves. She untied the bandanna, dipped it into the water, and wiped her face and neck of sweat and dust.

A slap against the water caused her to look up quickly. She watched a beaver resurface and scramble onto flattened ground where a cluster of poplar trees grew, several of which sported notches from the creature's gnawing. The beaver had squinted slits for eyes and crinkly bare ears. It stood up on it's hind legs and tipped its nose upward to detect any possible danger. As its nose wiggled up and down, it showed off four curved teeth stained as if from eons of continuous tobacco chewing. Eventually it ambled back into the water and disappeared.

Mayme checked the saddle girth and gathered the reins. Duster seemed refreshed from her long drink and short rest. The sweat on her neck had dried and Mayme made a mental note to give her a good brush down when she camped for the night.

The trees ahead were dense and green. "I better take advantage of the sun while we still have it, eh girl?" Duster pricked her ears forward and seemed to listen. Mayme slid the pocket watch out and checked the map against her current position. "So far, so good."

A few minutes later she wove Duster through the stand of cottonwoods lining the river. The ground slowly rose as she rode. She knew she must be close to, if not into the foothills. The landscape was quite pleasing. The foliage was lush and shadows dappled the ground.

Eventually the water loving trees gave in to the pines. The ground was littered with brown needles and the tops of the trees stretched up tall into the sky. She came to an edge where the trees emptied out into a meadow covered in blooming flowers. As she took in the colorful landscape, her eyes came to rest at the base of the huge pine next to where Duster stood. A litter of pinecone flakes on the ground betrayed the red squirrel sleeping on the branch above. With its tufted ears and tail of fine hairs curled over its back and projecting just in front of its face, it resembled a large, hairy pinecone.

Duster tossed her head and stared intently across the meadow. Her big chest expanded as she took in a deep breath and fidgeted beneath Mayme. She put her hand on Duster's neck and squinted to try to see what had her horse's attention. She thought she might have seen some shadows and maybe a glint of something shiny, but in the end, she couldn't be sure. Besides, whatever it was must have moved on because Duster snorted once and lowered her head to grab a few mouthfuls of grass.

Mayme loosened the strap on the rifle scabbard just in case. She knew Indians lived in this part of the country, although she'd ever laid eyes on one, even in town. Then again, it very well may have been the stallion that Mr. Smart had spoken of. If it came down to preventing him from stealing Duster and shooting him, she didn't think she would hesitate. Suddenly she realized exactly how Mr. Smart felt.

The sun touched the peaks of the mountains and was starting its slow decent into night. Slivers of bright orange and red streaked across the sky.

Mayme had already made her first mistake. She'd forgotten how quickly it got dark after the sun disappeared behind the mountains. She scanned the meadow. Other than a few taller flowers moving in the slight breeze, all was still.

She dismounted and quickly got to work. After looping a rein over a low branch, she loosened the girth and slid the saddle off Duster's back. She untied her bedroll and saddlebag and put them next to a downed log. Realizing she needed to get a fire going quickly, she scraped the ground of litter and scuffed as much dirt to the sides as possible. There wasn't much because of the deeply imbedded granite, but it would suffice. She snapped dead branches off the pines and soon had a decent pile.

The flint was easy to use. With the dry tinder, the sparks caught hold and soon small flames licked the wood. The pine resin snapped as it burned and reminded Mayme of the fires she used to build for cooking at Mrs. Randall's house.

That thought brought about a pang of loneliness. She missed Iris' and Mr. Smart's company. They both had added so much value to her life. There was no doubt in her mind that she wouldn't have succeeded in getting this job if it weren't for their help. Her fatigue would make her long for their company more, she knew, so she focused on caring for

Duster and making something to eat. She was tired enough that sleep wouldn't be long in coming afterward.

Mayme woke suddenly to impenetrable darkness. The fire had died down to embers so the only light was the bit that crept from the moon through the tree canopy. Duster's dark form remained motionless, although her head was up and alert with ears pricked forward. Mayme strained to look through the darkness, but to no avail.

An owl hooted from across the meadow and was answered by another from the trees behind her. Other than that, all was quiet. But what woke her? And what had Duster's attention? Mayme's heart beat thickly in her ears. She was sure even Duster could hear it. She slid her hand out from under the blanket and felt for the rifle. She'd propped it against the saddle before she'd gone to bed. A surge of panic was nearly her undoing as she failed to find the gun. Her fingers finally landed on it as she bent her elbow and felt nearer to her head. She rolled her eyes, thinking this was all ridiculous. But Duster's sudden snort told her differently.

Mayme fought the instinct to freeze. With a shaky hand, she slid the rifle down along her ribs and held it to her chest. She closed her eyes and took a deep breath. Beads of sweat formed on her upper lip and she licked it nervously. As slowly as she could, she shoved the blanket off to the side and rolled into a deeper shadow, one where what was left of the fire couldn't touch. She crept forward on her hands and knees until she crouched by Duster's front legs.

Duster lowered her head and blew a soft breath into Mayme's hair.

"Easy girl," Mayme whispered.

Uneventful minutes turned into what seemed like hours. Her knees ached from maintaining her position. She finally gave in and sat down. She draped the rifle over her lap and leaned against the tree to which Duster was tied.

A bird woke her once again, although this time it wasn't an owl. In fact the meadow and woods around her was full of birdsong. Robins, magpies, and chickadees flitted among the branches above her.

She couldn't believe she fell asleep. Her butt was asleep and she was sure she had the bark imprint on her cheek. Her muscles ached from the tension of last night and riding all day yesterday.

Duster wiggled her lip over the top of Mayme's head.

"Some help you are. You let me fall asleep, you big oaf." Mayme got to her feet and stroked the mare's neck. Dried, crusty sweat flaked under her hand and she instantly felt guilty for not giving Duster the grooming she'd promised.

After surveying the expanse of the meadow for any movement, Mayme grabbed handfuls of pine needles and rubbed them over Duster's hide. After she finished a little while later, Duster's coat was smooth and shiny. Mayme untied her and with the rope dragging at her feet, Duster grazed the grasses nearby. She was quite pleased to see the mare didn't seem to want to wander too far.

Breakfast consisted of some of the fried bread Iris had given her and a can of beans. She'd been so engrossed in navigating the countryside on horseback that she'd only eaten a few bites of jerky yesterday. She made a mental vow not to do that again as it added to her fatigue and could ultimately be deadly if her reaction time was slowed.

While chewing the last mouthful of bread, she wound the watch and confirmed her route for the day. After making sure the fire was completely dead, she readied Duster, gathered everything, and tied it onto the saddle.

Her route would take her into the southern side of the meadow. Curiosity got the better of her so she decided to ride to the meadow's far side before taking the prescribed way out.

Mayme watched Duster's ears and paid particular attention to her body language as they crossed the meadow. Aside from a few hard tail swishes, she didn't seem to be bothered by anything. But her blood chilled as she saw the large area of flattened grass. She looked around as she slid the rifle from the scabbard. Everything was still. Even the birds had quieted. The hairs on the back of her neck stood up and she felt like she was being watched. She zig-zagged Duster back and forth looking for clues but saw nothing that hinted at what had been here.

Deciding she'd wasted enough time looking for what well could be nothing at all, she pointed Duster toward the intended course and eased her into a canter. The further she got from that spot, the more at ease she felt.

She just reached the edge of the meadow, about to enter the trees and heard an owl hoot. She pulled Duster up fast, turned around, and scanned the tree line. Owls were normally quiet during the day. Something wasn't right. Whatever or whoever was out there was well hidden and had no desire to be seen.

She gathered the reins and squeezed her legs into Duster's sides. It seemed Duster was just as anxious to leave because she half-reared and pushed off with her hindquarters.

A light mist settled over the mountains as they climbed higher and the trees grew shorter. The horizon to the east was clear and several rays of sun speared their way out of the clouds. It seemed a vast silence reigned over the land.

Mayme looked behind her every few minutes for the first two hours. But eventually her neck grew tired of the harsh twisting and every time she turned, Duster reacted to her weight adjustment in the stirrups. She'd had to check the pocket watch a couple times to make sure they were still on course.

The trees eventually fell away to a huge meadow that occupied the entire side of a mountain. Jagged boulders of granite sporadically littered it. The cloud deck had finally risen to reveal the vast mountain range. She suddenly felt very small and alone, and patted Duster's neck for reassurance.

She pointed Duster downhill toward a flatter ridge, which seemed to circle the mountain. According to the map, this would take her northwest and within a day's ride of Oro Fino Creek.

Two brown ptarmigan, small chicken-like birds, skittered like moving shadows through the short plants. They crossed in front of them and finally took to the air on stiff wings.

A golden eagle screamed from above. As Mayme brought

her gaze down from the sky, one of the boulders moved. No, not a boulder. Her heart caught in her throat as she realized it was a grizzly bear.

Thankfully the bear was occupied, busily eating berries and seemingly anything else it could find. It had a massive head, concave facial profile, and small ears. Its high shoulders produced a sloping back, which emphasized its robust build. The light-colored shaggy coat glimmered in the sun as it moved. It casually turned its head and caught sight of her and Duster. It watched them for a few moments before rising up on its hind legs. The high shoulder hump was more visible and Mayme saw the mass of powerful muscles that drove the front legs. Six-inch daggers for claws hung from its paws.

She silently urged Duster on and left the bear to fill its stomach with the berries and not fresh meat.

The hours passed without event. By mid-day she'd descended the mountain far enough to meet up with a fast-rushing creek. According to the map, this was Oro Fino Creek. Tomorrow she'd need only to follow the creek upstream and make her first mail delivery.

Once she made camp, gathered firewood, and had a low fire burning, she led Duster to the creek. She wetted the now empty sack Iris had given her and rubbed it over Duster's hide. Dirt, sweat, and hair ran down her legs and were swept away by the water.

Mayme drank in the fragrance of the cool water. By the time she was done with Duster, she was anxious to clean off her own sweat and dirt, in addition to that of Duster's that clung to her.

While Duster grazed the lush grasses along the stream, Mayme shed her clothes. She breathed a sigh of relief upon removing the wrap from her chest. She was chaffed in a few places, but nothing severe.

Finally naked, she didn't hesitate to submerge herself into a quiet pool beneath a tree, which had at one time lost the fight against an eroding torrent. Although the water was chilly and goose flesh peppered her skin, it was quite refreshing. She used the sandy silt from the creek bottom to scrub the dirt and grime from her body. The cold eventually drove her out and she stood by the fire to dry and get warm. Her last chore before settling down to eat was to rinse her shirt and wrap, and hang them by the fire to dry.

Mayme kept her eye on Duster. She'd come to trust her to alert her to any danger. But the horse seemed content to graze. Every once in a while she'd raise her head with a mouthful of grass and watch Mayme work around camp.

Before she retired for the night, Mayme tied Duster close. This time she laid the rifle right alongside her instead of propping it against the saddle.

Duster's nicker woke her later when the moon was high in the sky. She flung the blanket back, grabbed the rifle, and stood by Dusters side.

"What is it, girl?" She laid her hand on Duster's neck. The horse seemed more curious than nervous. She heard horses stepping among the rocks somewhere downstream, heard them drink from the shallow pools in the dark where the rocks lay smooth. Eventually all was quiet.

She stood for a while longer and hearing nothing, returned to her bedroll. She still kept the rifle close. As she lay here, she wondered if the horses belonged to the stallion Mr Smart had spoken of. Would he have driven his herd this far into the mountains? But, she reasoned, if that were the case, why hadn't the stallion tried to drive Duster away?

Sleep claimed her again before she came to any conclusions. Aside from a few minor snaps as the fire cooled down, the only sound was that of the moving water.

Chapter Fifteen

THE TOWN, IF one could call it that, of Oro Fino Creek, seemed scattered about as if the buildings sprang up sporadically wherever the builder deemed a decent spot.

As she rode past the saloon, she noticed thick boards, like horizontal shutters propped up by poles above all the windows. Each one had a three-inch hole cut into the center. She wondered the purpose until she arrived in front of the post office and saw two arrows embedded in one of them. It suddenly became clear. The shutters were let down for protection in case of an Indian ambush. The holes must be where the residents poked their rifle barrels out and shot at their attackers.

She tied Duster at the hitching post and took the mochila into the post office. Unlike the one in Eagle Rock, the interior was nearly bare except for a desk and a few wooden boxes stacked next to it.

"Ah, our first mail delivery. How exciting." A thin gray-haired man with crooked legs stood up painfully and met Mayme halfway. "You must be Nathan. I received a telegraph enquiring whether you'd made it or not."

"Yes, sir. I rode as fast as I could, having never been on this route before." Mayme surrendered the bag to him. "I reckon I'll be faster next time."

"Well, you did just fine. The people here will be so relieved to know we have a dependable carrier."

Mayme smiled. "Is there anything you'd like for me to take back to Eagle Rock?"

"I can't answer that just yet. What I would suggest is that you put yourself up in the saloon for a day or two and rest your horse. I'll put the word out that you're in town. Check back with me day after tomorrow and I'll see what I have for you."

"Yes, sir. Thank you, sir." Mayme took a few steps toward the door and stopped short. "Do the Indians attack often? I noticed some arrows in the shutters outside."

The man took on a grim look. "Sadly, it seems like it's a monthly occurrence. Damned savages. Pardon my language. Seems like all they want to do is run through and see if they can take some scalps."

"I'm sorry to hear that."

"They've killed some mighty fine people."

Mayme walked out, feeling a mixture of hate and horror for the red men who took lives without reason. Savages indeed.

She led Duster to the livery and arranged for a stall. The owner refused any payment upon discovering she was the post rider.

Duster nickered to her as she turned to leave the barn with her saddlebags hanging over her shoulder.

"I know, girl. You'll be fine here. I'll check on you after I get myself a room and have something to eat." Mayme felt a bit guilty for leaving Duster. The horse had been a loyal companion and faithful guardian. But, as the postman said, both she and Duster needed rest and feed.

A red façade with cursive writing heralded her arrival at Big Nosed Kitty's saloon. A pair of "batwing" doors at the entrance hung on long hinges and extended from chest to knee level.

Mayme had never been in a saloon before. In fact, she had always crossed the street in Eagle Rock to avoid the smells of cigars and stale alcohol. In this case, she had no choice but to go inside.

The interior was a crude affair with minimal furniture and few decorations. A gray wolf hide hung behind the bar above the row of whiskey bottles. Four vacant tables and chairs stood on either side of the doorway. Seven stools were tucked under the overhang of the bar. A single wood-burning stove sat at the base of the stairs. No doubt so the warmth could be shared in the rooms above.

A very large, bespectacled man stood behind the bar,

wiping freshly washed glasses. He had full sideburns and eyes that spoke of seeing many things. He perused Mayme with open curiosity as she approached.

"You're new in these parts." He put the glass he'd dried on the counter. "What can I get you?" He lifted a whiskey bottled and motioned toward it.

Mayme shook her head quickly. "The postmaster told me to come here and enquire about a room." She noticed a sign advertising a free meal with the purchase of a drink. She pointed with her chin. "Does that apply to any meal?"

"Yep. Sure does. What's your pleasure?"

"I think I'd like to get a room first," she said wearily. "I'll come down when I get settled."

"Righto. How long you staying? We've got weekly rates, or if you think you'll be here longer, there's a boarding place down the road a spell. Ain't fancy, but it'd be a roof over your head."

"Two nights here will be fine. Thanks."

"The name's Miles in case you need anything."

Mayme started toward the stairs. "No, there's nothing I need at the moment."

The room Mayme chose on the second floor closely resembled the one she'd occupied at Mrs. Randall's. A single chest of drawers stood against the wall with a round mirror nailed above it. A washbasin, a full pitcher of water, and lamp were the only items on the roughly hewn surface.

A single casement window allowed light in as she parted the dingy curtains. A few horse and riders rode past the buildings, but other than that, all was quiet. She wondered if the town's inhabitants were still out working in the gold fields.

She went to the bed, kicked off her boots, tossed her hat onto the dresser, and stretched out on top of the covers. The cotton mattress felt wonderful after sleeping on the hard ground. In a few moments she was asleep.

Mayme's pocket watch read a few minutes after eight. She couldn't believe she'd slept so long. The last vestiges of daylight had been replaced by splinters of moonlight that penetrated the curtains.

Voices from below mingled together to create a dull roar that rose and lowered in tempo like the ebb and flow of waves on a lake.

Her stomach grumbled and reminded her that she hadn't eaten anything since a quick breakfast on the trail. She rubbed her eyes and poured water into the basin. She caught sight of herself in the mirror, and very nearly didn't recognize the figure that reflected back. Her face sagged with the fatigue of days on the trail and the stress of entering the unknown. She ruffled her hair and then pasted it in place with damp hands after splashing her face.

Feeling more awake now, and even hungrier, she ventured out.

She stood at the top of the stairs and surveyed the floor. The saloon was nearly full with men drinking at the bar or tables. Some were apparently asleep with their heads resting on folded arms. Others played cards, still others were enjoying a hot meal. A silver haze from smoke clung to the ceiling, moving only when someone came in from outside.

In the far corner, a scantily clothed woman stood next to a seated man. She looked around as if bored while he fondled her breasts with one hand and stroked her backside with the other. Something about her seemed familiar, but in the poor light, Mayme couldn't be sure.

There was one empty stool next to the bar and it was there she headed. The seat next to it was comfortably far enough away and occupied by one of the sleeping men.

"Ready for that meal now?" Miles wiped the surface in front of her with a rag that long ago must have been white.

"Yes, sir."

"You have your choice tonight. Boiled elk roast and mashed taters or boiled elk roast and mashed taters." A well-hidden grin raised his moustache.

Mayme chuckled and shrugged. "Hard choice, but I think I'll have the elk and potatoes. Could I please just have some water with that?"

"Not a drinker?"

"My horse hates the smell of it." Mayme smiled at her little white lie. "And I'm not allowed to drink. Boss's orders."

"I see." The bartender poured a glass of water and expertly slid it to her waiting hands. "I'll put your order in. It shouldn't be long."

MAYME SIPPED FROM her glass and spun around to put her back against the bar. She stole glances at the various patrons, but her gaze kept flitting back to the woman she'd seen from the upstairs floor. As she was now in better light, Mayme could see the woman had crimson hair, but so far she hadn't been able to get a good look at her face.

The man who'd been fondling her had apparently lost interest in her. He'd gotten to his feet, albeit unsteadily, and was heading in the direction of a younger girl on the other side of the room.

"Here you go, young fella. Eat 'em up."

Mayme turned as Miles placed the plate full of aromatic food in front of her. Her mouth watered in anticipation and she eagerly picked up the knife and fork. She closed her eyes and hummed when she put the first mouthful of sweet meat into her mouth.

"Now that's what I like to see. A young man enjoying his food."

Mayme shoved in another mouthful and looked toward the voice. *Betty!* She gasped and a piece of meat lodged in her throat. She doubled over, and while the woman thumped her on the back, she choked and gagged until the errant lump dropped onto the floor.

"Land sakes, are you all right?"

Mayme nodded but kept her head down. She did but she didn't want to look up at the woman who she'd recognized. The same Betty she'd met on the train months earlier. The one person in this town who stood a chance of recognizing her.

"Miles, get him something stronger to drink. Put it on my tab."

"Sure thing, Kitty."

Kitty? Mayme shook her head. "Thanks, but no. I'm okay." Her voice was raspy and she had a hard time keeping it in character of Nathan. She had no idea how she was going to handle this if Betty didn't leave soon.

Betty shot her a strange look. "Never mind. Bring his food and a tall glass of water to my room. Bring a scotch for me, please."

"Yes, ma'am."

Betty grasped Mayme by the arm. "Come with me."

She allowed herself to be led upstairs and through a door that went into a different section of the building. Betty stopped at door number five and removed a key from her bodice. Mayme worked to keep from smiling. Betty's safe.

Betty unlocked the door, pulled Mayme inside, and latched the door.

Mayme took in the surroundings. There was a bed in one corner, in another a stove, a coal hod, and a bundle of kindling sitting near it. A small dresser with a washbasin was pushed against the wall. Permeating everything was a mixture of disinfectant, hair oil, and cheap perfume. A few pictures hung on the walls, oddly enough, with innocent scenes of flowers and mountains.

"I never in a million years expected to see you here, let alone in a saloon."

Mayme turned and for the first time, looked openly at Betty. Her red dress was nearly as fancy as a ball gown. Its elaborate lace stitching flowed down the neckline. Silken laces so fine, they barely seemed to contain Betty's bust. A decorative braid wrapped tightly around her waist and accentuated her voluptuous curves.

"I thought you were headed to California. And why did Miles call you Kitty?"

Betty sighed and pointed to her bed.

Mayme hesitated.

"Please. Sit. We have a lot to catch up on."

There was a knock on the door. Betty opened it and took

the platter holding Mayme's food and the drinks. "Thanks, Miles. Please make sure I'm not disturbed for a few hours."

Miles winked. "Sure thing."

Betty latched the door and set the platter on her dresser. "Here." She handed Mayme her plate of food. "You eat, I'll talk. Then I want to know why you're dressed as a young man in a rough mining town."

"Okay." Mayme sliced a piece of meat and put it in her mouth. The food had cooled but was still very edible.

"I never made it to California like I'd planned. When the train stopped in Salt Lake City, I received word that Oro Fino Creek had need of a saloon proprietor. It took me a month to gather enough money, but I was finally able to make my way back to Idaho."

Mayme widened her eyes. "Only a month?"

Betty raised her chin slightly. "Yes, well, I'm a good business woman if I say so myself."

Mayme recalled what she'd seen earlier and it became clear. Very clear.

"You're a prostitute."

"I prefer painted lady." Betty flicked imaginary dust off her lap. Her long nails caused lines in the dress fabric.

"Why does Miles call you Kitty?"

Betty frowned. "Women like me are not always looked upon with approval. Especially when some of the men that frequent a brothel are married. So it's not uncommon for a painted lady to change her name when she relocates."

"I see."

"You don't think less of me, do you, Mayme?" Betty's lower lip protruded in a small pout.

"Of course not. I don't quite understand why you would allow someone to grope you the way I saw that man did earlier. But to each their own, I guess."

"You have to understand that jobs are far and few out here. Some women lose their husbands and have no family or money, or sometimes their families would ask them to leave home, and if they have no place to go, or no skills, they have only one answer."

"Which one were you?"

Betty threw her head back and laughed. "I, my dear, chose this profession for a life of adventure." She leaned in and whispered conspiratorially, "And to escape the rules of women behaviour. I simply hate being told what to do, what to wear, how to behave." She took Mayme's empty plate and set it on the dresser, then traded it for Mayme's glass of water and her scotch. "Your turn. What have you done and who's after you?"

Her question made Mayme laugh. "Nobody is after me and aside from a few white lies, I haven't done anything wrong." When she finished relating her story to Betty, who she now had to refer to as Kitty at Betty's request, she took a deep breath and waited.

Kitty stared at her for a moment and then shook her head.

"So what you're telling me is that the money I gave you is stalled in the livery."

"Yes. I'll pay you back as—"

"No. You absolutely will not." A devilish grin narrowed her painted lips. "I love that you're fooling all those egotistical idiots out there who think everything but cooking, cleaning, and child birthing is man's work. Will this be your regular route?"

"According to Lawrence, my boss in Eagle Rock, it should be."

Kitty patted her lap with glee. "Excellent. I insist you stay here every time."

"Um. In your room? What if you're—?"

"Don't be silly. I'll have Miles set one up for you before you come back."

Chapter Sixteen

MAYME DRAPED THE mochila over her shoulder, threw her right leg over Duster's neck, and slid to the ground. She felt quite pleased with herself and Duster. Although this had only been her fourth trip through the mountains, she'd been able to reduce her travel time between Eagle Rock and Oro Fino Creek by an entire day.

She trotted up the few steps to the post office and waited patiently as the postmaster she now knew as Gerald, finished waiting on an elderly man.

"Well, well, well. Look who's back in town." Gerald ran his finger over the numbers on the calendar that hung on the wall behind him. He turned to her with surprise on his face. "You weren't due here until late tomorrow, early the next day."

"I know." Mayme couldn't temper the grin of satisfaction. "I'm getting used to the route. Plus, I was kind of hoping I could get a new set of shoes on Duster while I'm here. It's best if she has them on for a day or two before I head off again."

"Very well. I'll not schedule you for a couple days then. Good job, Nathan."

FLUFFY WHITE SUDS and delicious warm water covered Mayme up to her neck. Much to her delight, Kitty arranged a bath for her every time she rode into town and she loved soaking in it. The pain of sore muscles from long hard hours in the saddle dissipated, as did the grime off her body.

A short rap on the door preceded Kitty's entrance into the room with towels and a tin of salve.

"Are you finished turning yourself into a prune?" Kitty laid a towel on the floor next to the tub.

"Yeah. The water is getting cold anyway." Mayme pushed the remaining suds to the side and stood up. She still felt a little shy about being naked in front of Kitty, but slowly that was being dispelled by a familiarity they shared with each other.

"That's what happens when winter is nearing. Your baths will get shorter and shorter from here on out. Sometimes you'll feel like you should just jump in and out and dry off." Kitty politely averted her eyes and handed Mayme a large rough towel. "Okay, now turn around and let me see how bad your chaffing is this time."

Mayme turned her back to Kitty and continued to dry herself.

"It's looking better but I'm going to put some more of this bloodroot on. It seems the worst of it was under your arms, but even that doesn't look as angry anymore." With soft gentle strokes, she applied the red ointment.

"I think I'll be okay once my skin gets used to wearing that wrap." Mayme reached for the loose cotton shirt she wore only when there wasn't any chance of being seen. Although the shirt was baggy, she wasn't about to take any chances of having her true sex discovered.

"How long are you here for this time?" Kitty twisted the lid down on the container and set it on the small table next to the tub.

"Two days. Duster needs new shoes and could use the rest. I've been pushing her pretty hard." She slipped the shirt over her head and reached for her trousers.

"I think that goes for you too. It's going to get harder to navigate those mountains once the snow flies."

Mayme sighed and nodded. "I've been watching where the elk move. I think I'll be able to use their trails when the snow gets deep."

"I still think it's going to be a challenge for you. It would be for anyone really. Ready for something to eat? I'll bring it up so you don't have to worry about being seen."

"Thanks. I'm starved."

MAYME WOKE JUST after dawn, dressed quickly, and headed outside. Cold air streamed down from the mountaintops. There was a metallic smell about the air, indicative of an early snowfall.

She pushed her hat firmly on her head and wrapped her coat closer to her sides. The town was quiet except for the nickering of hungry horses in the livery. She was sure Duster was amongst the most demanding.

The smell of what seemed like a burnt honey and sulphur mixture got stronger as she neared the building. The blacksmith was already preparing his hot forge for a day of shoeing horses. The clanking of a hammer, the first one sharp, and then several descending, signalled he was shaping a shoe on the anvil.

The blacksmith had no one else scheduled until late morning, so Mayme interrupted Duster's breakfast and tied her to the hitching post.

"You're that post rider, ain't you?"

"Yes, sir."

The blacksmith removed Duster's thin, worn out shoes and trimmed each hoof. "Your horse has a few stone bruises, young fella. Do you have a backup horse?"

"No, sir." Mayme peered at Duster's right front hoof. Two reddish blotches, one on the toe and the other near the tip of Duster's frog, stood out against the newly parred white sole. "They don't look too bad. Can you put a poultice underneath a leather pad?"

The blacksmith raised his eyebrows. "You're from out east, ain't you? I've only ever heard of them rich people doing that to their horses."

Mayme squirmed under his scrutiny. Should she add another white lie to the growing list?

He let go of Duster's foot and scrubbed his chin. "Aw, it don't matter anyway. Thing is, we need to keep your mare comfortable. You're just lucky I know how to do it proper like. Leave her with me a bit and I'll take care of them hooves. I'll put her back in the stall when I'm done."

ON HER WAY back to the saloon, she heard her name called. She looked behind her and saw Gerald jogging toward her.

"Nathan," he said before doubling over, out of breath. He pointed a finger upward to indicate she should wait. He finally straightened up and swiped his brow. "I'm glad I caught you. A wire came in for you." He handed her a sweaty and crumpled piece of paper. "Sounds like you might have to ride out of here sooner."

Mayme smoothed the square message flat on her hand. It was titled post office telegram with a priority stamp on the top. She smiled knowing Gerald was being ever official. But the smile evaporated as she read.

> *Nathan Adams. Abandon mail carry duties at once. Post rider missing since last week. Search area between Greer and Kamiah. Notify asap as to whereabouts of William Prescott.*

"Billy? Billy is missing?" She bounced a curled knuckle against her mouth.

"You know him?"

She'd forgotten Gerald was there. "Oh. Um, yeah. I know him. Not well. But enough to know it'd take a lot for him to go missing."

"You better load up on ammo. You'll be going right into the heart of Injun country. Those mountains aren't the kindest either."

"How far from Oro Fino is Greer?"

"You're looking at a two days ride at least. The country is rough. Then it's another three, if you're lucky, to Kamiah. A lot of slow, hard riding."

Mayme sighed, ticking off in her head the supplies she'd need. She looked back toward the livery and made a silent plea that Duster would be able to handle navigating the rough country on her sore feet. She certainly had enough money saved for another horse. But she trusted Duster with her life and she knew she could count on her to keep her safe. If worse came to worst, she'd lead Duster to make the travel easier on her.

"Okay. Return a telegraph stating I'll be leaving tomorrow morning at daybreak." At least, she thought, Duster's feet would have another twenty-four hours to heal.

KITTY WAS FAR from happy when Mayme told her.

"But why do *you* have to go?" Kitty paced back and forth. The swishing of her dress matched the tempo of her heels tapping the floor.

"I imagine because I'm closer than any other rider." Mayme shoved sacks of biscuits, jerky, and a few cans of tomatoes and peaches into one side of the saddlebag. She'd already filled the other side with three pounds of oats and her clothing on top.

"I don't care. It'll be too dangerous for you."

"Why? Because I'm a girl?"

"No! All right, yes. I suppose that's the main part of it." Kitty grasped Mayme's arms and squeezed. "That country is no place for a girl to be. It's rough and it seems the Indians have been murdering every white man they come across."

"Then I guess it's a good thing I am a girl."

"You're not funny." Kitty released her and started pacing again.

Mayme secured the straps on the saddlebags and set them to the side. She put her hands on her hips. "Look, if I don't do this, all my riding credibility will be gone. They'll get suspicious. If I'm able to ride my route through some pretty rough country why would I baulk at their request?" She paused for a moment. "Plus, I know the boy who's missing."

Kitty's eyebrows disappeared into her hair. "Oh. Might we have a crush on said boy?"

Mayme snorted. "Hardly. He's a pompous ass."

"Then why?"

"Because, even though I can't reveal my identity to him when I find him, I'll get a lot of self-satisfaction that I've bettered him. He belittled me a few times at the mercantile."

"A vendetta? You're willing to risk your life to prove a point." Kitty flung her hands into the air. "Mayme, I don't understand you. But you've obviously made up your mind to do something crazy. Again. I guess I can't stop you. Just promise me you'll return safely."

Mayme wrapped her arms around Kitty. "I promise I'll come back safe and sound."

THE ONLY LIGHT in the sky came from the moon as Mayme walked to the livery the next morning. She'd planned on getting up early, but according to the pocket watch, which she dutifully wound, it'd only been four am. Nerves, excitement, determination, and fear began battling one another as soon as she'd opened her eyes. She gave up, knowing there was no use in trying to get back to sleep for only an hour.

Duster nickered a greeting as she opened the barn door. The only other occupants were an old mule and a pair of oxen. None of them paid her any attention until she tossed some hay into Duster's stall for the mare to eat while she saddled her. After slinging a few forkfuls of hay into the other stalls, she finished tacking Duster up. Since it was still early, she refrained from putting the bridle on until Duster pulled the last small portion into her mouth.

Mayme checked for heat in all four hooves. Finding them cool set her more at ease.

"All right, big girl. We have an important mission this time. More crucial than delivering the mail. Billy's life may be at stake."

Duster nudged her shoulder.

"Yes, I know he's an idiot. But even so, we have to find him."

Rays of the upcoming sun splayed over the mountaintops as she led Duster out of the barn. She made the horse circle her in both directions to check for any hint of lameness. Seeing none, she crossed the reins over Duster's neck, put her foot into the stirrup, stepped up, and swung her right leg over.

The first few miles were familiar, but thereafter she had to navigate directly south. Some of her route took her along the pebble-lined banks of Oro Fino Creek. But the walls on either side eventually grew too sheer to climb. She backtracked until she found a place that wasn't too dangerous. To make it as easy as possible on Duster, she navigated hairpin turns all the way up until the terrain evened out as much as it could on the side of the mountain. The higher she rode, the colder it got. She waited until Duster needed a breather before she pulled the horse up and donned her coat. By then she was chilled to the bone. A cold breeze descended from the mountain and dried the sweat she'd worked up while riding.

Mayme's teeth started chattering, and she decided it was time to find a spot to camp and warm up by a fire. She'd be no use to Billy if she caught pneumonia. She remembered Maddie had often referred to it as "the old man's friend" because it would carry away the old folks who couldn't look out for themselves anymore.

An outcropping of huge boulders burst its way into the forest. Old growth hemlock stood vigil over them. She nearly missed seeing a small cave partially hidden in the deep shadows.

Mr. Smart had warned her that mountain lions preferred this sort of habitat. Mayme slid the rifle out of the scabbard and cautiously rode closer. There were no visible impressions in the pine litter or disturbed ground where a lion might bring a kill to feed her cubs. Still, she remained cautious until she realized Duster showed no sign of a predator being near.

Mayme dismounted with the rifle in one hand and the reins in the other. Despite Duster being reliable, she'd heard too many stories of horses getting spooked, running off, and stranding their riders. She wasn't about to take that chance.

But she soon realized she didn't have to worry about the four-legged residents of these mountains. A fire-ring made of variously sized rocks was tucked between two boulders just outside and to the right of the cave opening. As expected, the half-burned wood and resulting ash was cold. It didn't appear as if it had been used in a long time, or more than once. There was no pile of wood anywhere, which might have indicated an intended return by the previous inhabitant.

Satisfied it was a safe enough area and that she was completely alone, Mayme finally relaxed and made camp. It was easy enough to find sufficient firewood from the dead lower branches of the pines. They crackled into a hot blaze. She gave Duster a few healthy handfuls of oats to eat. She'd tied her with enough rope length to nibble on the sparse grass growing wherever a bit of light could make its way through the canopy. After eating some jerky strips and a can of peaches, she banked the fire and turned in for the night.

A few owls called to one another from different directions. The echoes of their calls gave the mountains an eerie feeling.

Mayme's thoughts wandered to Billy for the first time since early morning. She'd been so busy focusing on Duster and finding a navigable way southward, her purpose had faded. Until now.

Why would Billy have disappeared? She couldn't believe he would just abandon his post without cause. He had been so excited that day in the mercantile. Maybe something happened to his horse. If so, more than likely he was on foot. Whatever the reason, it was her job to find him.

Chapter Seventeen

THE FIRE HAD gone out and a cold, saturating mist hovered above. Mayme knew the only way to get warm would be to get up and move. Still undecided, she lay there and looked at the sky through the narrow canopy of pine. Although it was getting light, Venus stubbornly remained in the sky.

Mayme glanced at Duster, who seemed perfectly comfortable despite the weather. She was busy nibbling the last of the grass. The mare had done well yesterday and hadn't missed a step. Hopefully the leather pads would continue to keep her sound.

rrrRRR-eee-EEE-UH-UH-UH-UH-uh

Mayme flung the blanket back and jumped to her feet. The loud, variably pitched scream had come from somewhere behind her.

rrrRRR-eee-EEE-UH-UH-UH-UH-uh

Oddly Duster didn't seem disturbed by the ear-piercing scream. Mayme held her rifle close and plastered herself against the rocks. The boulders became too small to give her sufficient cover, and she darted from tree to tree, the trunks of which were twice as wide as her body.

rrrRRR-eee-EEE-UH-UH-UH-UH-uh

Mayme was surprised to find that the forest emptied out into a huge meadow. She now recognized the dark brown animal. The bull elk had a buff-colored rump and long thin legs. His head, neck, belly, and legs were darker than his back and sides, and he sported a chestnut-brown neck and mane. A top his head was a set of massively sharp antlers.

rrrRRR-eee-EEE-UH-UH-UH-UH-uh

A second bull, equally as large, bugled a challenge and came forward. He raked his six-foot long antlers aggressively against a small pine tree and strutted toward his opponent.

They walked parallel to each other, seemingly to size each other up. They passed several times as if comparing each other's antlers, body size, and fighting prowess. Mayme watched in captivation. A movement at the tree edge revealed several cows watching the two bulls.

Suddenly the bulls faced each other, lowered their heads, and clashed their antlers together, locking them. They wrestled like this for several minutes before releasing and charging each other again. The sounds of the battle echoed throughout the woods. The cows remained motionless.

Finally the first bull drove his opponent off. Their sides heaved and both sported deep, bloody gouges in their hides. Only after the other bull retreated did the cows emerge and casually begin grazing.

The conflict had turned a formerly huge grassy area into churned-up dirt. The cold forgotten, Mayme had never seen anything like it. The power, the noise of the two bulls as they fought, grunted, and struggled was astonishing.

By now the sun had risen and all vestiges of the night were long gone. While she would've rather watched the herd of elk greet and mingle with their champion, she knew she had to make a move. Damn Billy.

She saddled Duster while nibbling a strap of jerky and taking small sips of water from her canteen. They'd have to find water today. One of the two canteens she carried was completely empty and the one she drank from now was only half full. Duster was in much need of water too.

She checked the watch against the map, and discovered her route would take her past the elk meadow, on a downhill slope and hopefully toward water. She gave Duster another handful of oats before mounting and riding off.

The litter of needles on the forest floor was a blessing and a detriment. It cushioned Duster's feet, but it also hid rocks on which she inevitably stumbled or slipped on. By the time Mayme found a narrow groove of a creek that yielded little water, they were both sweaty and tired.

Mayme climbed down and wiggled over two fallen trees to

fill the canteens. There was no easy and safe way to get Duster to the water. She took a pot out of the saddlebag, returned to the water and filled it. Duster eagerly emptied each of the twelve offered her.

Her legs felt like jelly by the time she finished hauling water. It was only mid-morning and they had a ways to go before the day ended. She ate another strip of jerky and checked the map while sitting at Duster's feet. Relief settled over her as she discovered she was close to the route Billy would've taken. She hoped to find a trail of some sorts and maybe a clue as to where he was.

Duster ate another handful of oats before Mayme stepped into the stirrup and climbed aboard. They picked their way down an easier slope and eventually came to where the infinitesimal creek she'd gotten water from earlier dripped into a larger flowing mass of water.

Mayme stood up in the stirrups at the river's edge and studied the moving water.

"Well, Duster, it looks like we're going to get wet."

Duster lowered her head and snorted at the rushing water. She stepped in and out of it a few times before moving forward. Mayme encouraged her by squeezing Duster's sides. She supported Duster's head with both reins to keep her moving straight.

Suddenly Duster lurched forward as the ground disappeared beneath her hooves. Water flowed up and over the saddle, drenching Mayme from the waist down and filling her boots. Duster lifted her nose over the water. Her nostrils flared as she paddled her way across.

The current pulled them downstream. Mayme found it hard to believe Duster was making any progress against the rushing water. She leaned forward and grasped Duster's mane.

"Come on, girl. You can do it."

Duster's ears twisted back and forth. She suddenly pitched forward and with one great shove from her hindquarters, found purchase on the river bottom. Half rearing, she pushed off again and cantered the remaining distance to the shore.

Mayme was soaked. The saddle and all her belongings in the saddlebags and the bedroll were saturated. There was no way she could avoid camping at the river's edge for the night. She needed to get dry before the cold set in or she'd be in dire straits.

Fortunately, the flint still worked and she soon had a roaring fire. There was no shortage of firewood. The river had deposited enough debris on its banks for a month of fires.

Mayme strung the rope between two trees and after wringing her clothing out, hung it downwind from the fire. The soft breeze produced by the rushing water pushed the warmth generated by the fire toward her garments.

The sun was bright and warm on the side they'd crossed to. She stood naked by the fire not caring if anyone saw her. Not that it was possible. She was in the middle of an uninhabited nowhere. Besides, if Billy were anywhere in the area, he wouldn't be able to refrain from saying anything.

When the light weighted garments dried she chose to put them on rather than wait for the heavier ones. Since her bedroll was made of wool, it took no time at all to dry. She decided to not put her chest wrap on until morning. The material was taking longer to dry and besides, it felt good to have it off for a change.

Duster grazed contentedly nearby. Since she'd used the rope to hold her clothes, she'd taken the reins off the bridle, tied them together and secured them around Duster's neck with one end drooping to the ground.

Mayme ate a dinner consisting of warmed tomatoes with some jerky thrown in for salt. It didn't take long for her eyelids to get heavy and the yawns to set in. Every muscle in her body was tired. She banked the fire and crawled into her bedroll. With the sound of the water in the background, she barely remembered closing her eyes.

A GOLDEN EAGLE'S scream from high above grabbed Mayme's attention late the next morning. She tugged on the reins and brought Duster to a halt. The eagle circled overhead, gradually rising higher, before it soared away in a southerly direction.

She'd started the ride by following the river. The banks were covered in small pebbles mixed with silt brought down by the melt high in the mountains. Every once in a while she had to ease Duster into the water to pass a boulder outcropping. Fortunately the water remained shallow with the deepest going to Dusters knees.

As she rounded the next bend, the river widened and became much shallower. The terrain had flattened out on either side into large expanses of prairie. Lush grass grew right to the water's edge.

She'd given Duster the rest of the oats while she'd eaten breakfast, but she knew the oats and sparse grass she'd nibbled in the mountains wasn't enough to satisfy her appetite.

Mayme guided Duster up the short bank and dropped the reins so she could graze for a while. In the meantime, she dismounted and refilled the water supply. She looped the canteen straps over the saddle horn and noticed a flock of black birds the size of pinpricks, circling in the blue sky about a mile away.

The wind carried the sound of a horse's neigh from the west. Duster flung her head up and answered. Half chewed grass fell from her mouth and she stared intently in the direction from which the sound had come. She whinnied again and was met with another neigh.

Mayme squinted and tried to find the location of the horse. She couldn't see anything, so decided to let Duster find it for her. It might be Billy. Mayme stepped up in the saddle and with loose reins, clucked to Duster, who needed no encouragement. She pushed off into a stiff-legged trot, head held high and ears pricked forward.

They eventually came to a brush-filled cove littered with river debris and rocks that had been pushed up by a flood. Young cottonwood trees had sprung up all around it, making the area nearly impenetrable.

Duster nickered loudly. A horse nickered back. Thrashing sounds came from the undergrowth. Mayme untied the rope and slid off the saddle. She looked for the easiest way in by circling around.

She finally located hoof prints in the sand that led into the brush. "How the heck did you get in there?"

Mayme shoved her way through by pushing the narrow trunks to the side. By the time she reached the horse, she was breathing hard and the mosquitos had found her. She barely noticed the whine of the pesky insects, nor the few bites as a couple descended on her for a meal. She brushed them away and approached the horse.

The chestnut gelding had four white socks and a white blaze painted down the front of its face. His hide was dull and speckled white with dried sweat. He wore a saddle and bridle of which one of the reins was broken off. He probably snapped it when he was running, Mayme speculated. The other was caught in the fork of a tree and wrapped so tightly around that the horse could barely move his head. The corner of the horse's mouth was raw and angry looking from the snagged rein working the bit.

As Mayme moved closer, the horse nickered softly to her and impatiently pawed the ground.

"Easy, boy. I'll get you out of here. Somehow." She draped the lariat over her head to free both hands and pushed her way to the gelding's side.

The saddle was scratched badly, but not enough to miss the widely lettered *BP* carved into the cantle. Could this be Billy's horse? Who else might have initials like that? But where was Billy? He certainly wasn't in the near vicinity, that's for sure.

It took Mayme a few minutes to free the remaining rein from the tree. She tried to turn the horse so she could backtrack in the direction she came. But the stirrups on both sides of the saddle caught firmly in the brush. The only way to get the horse out would be to leave the saddle behind.

She shook her head and rolled her eyes at the same time. "You'll just have to ride your horse bareback, Billy, you idiot.

Wherever you are." She was slightly amused that more than likely, Billy was walking around looking for his horse. But what had happened that his horse got frightened enough to run into someplace like this? Once again, she came back to the original question: Where *was* Billy?

As Mayme untied the latigo holding the girth and pulled the saddle off, she discovered a long shallow wound. The horses' hide was split, but the bleeding had since stopped.

"Poor boy. That's what you get for running into stuff like this."

It took twice as long for her to weave the gelding out of the brush than it did for her to enter it. And then they were finally free from the juxtaposed stand of trees.

Duster nickered as they came out and trotted over to smell the gelding. After Duster squealed a warning and stomped her foot, all was quiet.

The white in the gelding's eyes had disappeared and it was obvious he was much more relaxed.

Mayme fashioned a halter out of the rope and removed the bridle.

"That'll make you more comfortable, big guy."

She mounted Duster and ponied the gelding on her right side. After a trip to the river where both horses drank their fill they turned to the south. As they walked through the tall prairie grass, the horses nibbled on the tops. Oftentimes Mayme let them drop their heads to graze for a few minutes before continuing on.

The flock of birds, which earlier had been black dots in the sky, grew larger the farther south she rode. Finally recognizing them as vultures, a sense of foreboding overcame her. The fact she had Billy's horse in hand and so far there'd been no sign of boot prints, and therefore Billy, sent chills up and down her spine.

A vast silence reined over the land as she rode closer to the area the birds were circling. A slight breeze moved the grasses and every once in a while brought the smell of rankness with a tinge of sweetness. She recognized it as death. A few years prior, she'd been riding Blaze in the hills and came upon a dead cow. The smell was similar to that.

"Please be a dead cow. Please be a dead cow."

Although Mayme still hadn't spotted what lay in the grass ahead, she dismounted and ground tied Duster. She didn't want the smell to spook the horses. The gelding had already been through enough.

She slid the rifle out of the scabbard and walked forward with great reluctance.

The smell became so repugnant, it nearly knocked her backward. The buzz from what seems like millions of flies filled the air.

"Oh, God." She pulled her shirt up over her nose and held it tightly against her face. It did little to block the smell, but she knew she had no choice but to move forward.

Although Billy's body was riddled with arrows he still clutched his pistol. His formerly blue laughing eyes now stared sightlessly from his slack face. A dribble of blood had collected and dried at the corner of his mouth. His saddlebags lay behind his body. The mochila was draped over his lap. Large splotches of crimson stained the leather on both.

Mayme sighed heavily despite the smell. "Oh, Billy. Why'd you have to go and get yourself killed?"

Spent shells littered the ground everywhere. It was obvious he'd fought bravely. There were several other pools of blood in various places that'd been soaked up by the rain-starved ground. Drag marks were evident in the bent grasses where the fallen had been taken away.

"Looks like you held your own. I count one, two, three, four, five, six, maybe seven spots where they fell. At least they didn't scalp you."

Mayme realized she'd said more to Billy in death than she'd ever done in life. Horror turned to sadness and then indifference as she set about digging a grave with a battered pot from Billy's saddlebags. It couldn't be used for anything else. She'd had to pry an arrow out of it.

The sun was high and hot. There'd be no relief from passing

clouds as the air had become quite still. It wasn't long before her clothes pasted to her. Sweat streamed from her wrap and into the seam of her trousers. The brim of her hat was stained with a white streak as the sun dried her sweat from above.

It took the remainder of the day and the rest of the canteen water to dig the hole. In between scooping the deadpan soil and wiping sweat from her eyes, she stayed vigilant and scanned the area in case the Indians returned.

The smell was unbearable. She knew the longer Billy's body remained exposed, the worse it would get. The horses grazed nearby for a while, but even they moved farther away. If the gelding hadn't been tied to Duster, he would have run away as she approached for the canteens. She wore the smell of death.

The vultures circled lower. A sudden flap of wings gained her attention. One of the black birds had landed on Billy and another was on the ground not far from his body.

"Get out of here!" She picked up a rock and threw it at them. It bounced sickly against Billy's stomach. The bird hopped and landed again, this time on Billy's head. It bent its head over Billy's face and peered at him.

Mayme climbed out of the hole and ran toward the birds. "Leave him alone!"

The birds took to the air clumsily and with great objection. But they didn't return.

Mayme wiped her brow with her sleeve and looked back at the grave. All that time and it was barely three feet deep.

"I'm sorry, Billy. That's going to have to do. I just can't dig any deeper."

She pried the pistol from his hand. "You won't need this anymore. I hope you don't mind that I have it and not some Indian." She hefted it in her hand. "Bullets. SAAs." She frowned and wondered if he'd run out of ammunition before he died. She searched his saddlebags but didn't find a single unspent bullet.

"I guess you may as well keep this with you." Mayme placed it on Billy's chest and rubbed her hands together.

"Okay." She picked up his feet. "I don't expect you to make this easy." She grunted.

Billy looked lighter than he was. He was lean but very well muscled. With a series of jerks and then a couple breaks, she was able to drag him to the grave. She got the body parallel to it, held her breath, and rolled him into it. His head gave a hollow thump as it hit the hard ground.

"Oops. Sorry."

It took her another hour to scoop the dirt over him. Then she lined the grave with rocks she had dug up and draped his saddlebags over it.

"Don't worry. I'll deliver the mail this once for you."

It took some convincing to get Duster to let Mayme come close. Every time she'd get within five feet of the horses, they'd get a whiff of her and shy away. Maymc finally took her shirt and trousers off and was able to grab Duster's reins.

While holding the reins in one hand, she rolled her clothes into a tight wad and after a couple of attempts, mounted Duster. She rode straight to the river and took a well-earned and much-needed bath while the horses grazed nearby. Then she washed her clothes and laid them on the tops of the grass. They dried in short order and she was able to get dressed again. This time she had no trouble catching the horses.

It had been a long day and she was bone tired. Initially she thought she would camp at the previous night's site. But it was too late in the day to make that ride and frankly, she just didn't have the energy. So she opted to cross the river and found a suitable place upstream, one near some trees where she tied the horses. She was asleep before the moon rose.

Chapter Eighteen

THE NEXT MORNING, Mayme stared into the fire while gnawing on a piece of jerky. She was thinking about what to do next. Although Oro Fino Creek was the closest ride, the most logical route would be back to Eagle Rock. She could give Billy's mail filled mochila to Lawrence and let him decide what to do with it. More likely he'd send it to another post office via the train.

But that was the least of her worries. She'd have to relay the news of Billy's murder to Mr. Smart and for that her heart hurt. He was obviously quite fond of Billy. The combination of losing Billy might undo all the healing he'd done from losing his family.

Unfortunately, she had no choice. At this point in time, she was the only person on earth, aside from the Indians, that knew Billy was dead. Anyway, if truth were told, she thought Mr. Smart would rather hear it from her than someone else.

IT TOOK A week of hard riding to get to Eagle Rock. She'd had to do miles of back tracking. The terrain was difficult and challenging enough with one horse, let alone two. Billy's horse, who she'd named Red just to call him something, was a pain in the neck to pony. As long as he was beside Duster, he was fine. But when the trail became too narrow for two horses to pass side by side, he became a nightmare. He either lagged behind and tried to eat everything including the back of her saddle, or he'd try to push past Duster. Mayme tugged him back when he came up along her right side, but when he attempted it on the left he nearly unseated her. She was sorely tempted to just let him loose and offer him up to fate. But she worried he'd be an uncontrollable hazard on the trail if he decided to follow her.

Mayme had lost track of what day it was on the trail. She only knew how many nights it'd taken to get from one place to another. So she was a bit surprised as she rode up to the mercantile in Eagle Rock, only to find it closed.

"Huh. Must be Sunday."

Fortunately, it was early afternoon and she had plenty of time to get to Mr. Smart's farm before nightfall.

Mrs. Randall's house was quiet as she rode by. There wasn't a soul in sight. Mayme thought it odd if it was in fact Sunday. She, Iris, and Annie used to sit on the porch and amuse themselves by watching the Sunday traffic on the road. They'd take particular joy in watching the churchgoers file out and wait for the men to sneak back into town for a drink. Mayme had found no humor in this at first, but after listening to the quick wit of the other girls, she soon relaxed and joined the laughter.

Her horses and those of Mr. Smart greeted each other with loud whinnies. The noise of course alerted Mr. Smart. By the time she rode up to the house, he was waiting for her with hands on his hips and a huge smile that reached his eyes. It saddened her greatly, knowing her news would wipe it from his face.

"Well, look what the cat finally drug in. I expected you back last week. I was beginning to worry a spell."

Mayme smiled weakly and dismounted.

"I see you picked up another horse along the way. He's a beaut." Mr. Smart took Red's rope from her and looked at him with appreciation. "Nice stock. Very good legs. You done good."

"He's not mine."

Mr. Smart furrowed his eyebrows and then released them. "He's not?" He blinked twice and cocked his head. "Then whose is he?"

Mayme couldn't find any words that would make it easier on either of them. She took a deep breath and blew it out slowly. "He's Billy's"

Mr. Smart smiled quickly and looked around. "Billy is in town?"

"No. Damn. There's just no easy way to say this. The reason I was delayed is because I had to go find Billy."

"What do you mean?"

Mayme could see understanding building in his eyes, but she knew he had to hear the truth.

"When I got to Oro Fino Creek, I was told Billy was missing. Since I was the nearest available rider, I was asked to ride his route and see if I could find him. We all thought maybe his horse had gone lame or something and that Billy was on foot. But—"

Mr. Smart shook his head.

"I found him. I think he was ambushed by a bunch of Indians."

"Aw, Billy," Mr. Smart said sadly. His eyes welled up and a single tear worked its way down his cheek.

"He didn't go down without a fight. He used every last bullet and it looked like he killed a bunch of them."

Mr. Smart ran his hand through his hair. "They didn't—"

"He had his hair."

He closed his eyes and nodded before opening them again. "Then he was honored by them. Indians won't scalp or mutilate their enemies if they've fought well."

"Oro Fino Creek is having problems with them."

"It's the Blackfoot tribe."

"How do you know?"

"Because the damned government keeps taking away more and more of their land." Mr. Smart pulled a kerchief from his pocket, wiped his eyes, and blew his nose. He shoved it haphazardly into his back pocket. "Come on. Let's get these horses in the barn and you some grub."

MAYME LEFT MR. Smart's farm early the next morning. She needed to deliver Billy's mochila to the post office and receive the next assignment of mail for Oro Fino. She also hoped to catch a visit with Iris on her way.

Mrs. Randall was sweeping the front porch as Mayme rode up.

"Good morning." She reined Duster to a stop.

Mrs. Randall stilled the broom and shielded her eyes from the low sun.

"Oh, hello, Mayme. How nice to see you."

Mayme couldn't help but notice the monotone in her voice. Despite what she said, she didn't think Mrs. Randall was too happy to see her.

"I was hoping to see Iris. Is she around?" She stood up in the saddle and swung her right foot over the saddle and prepared to dismount.

"You may as well stay atop your horse. Iris isn't here."

"Oh. Okay." Mayme sat back down in the saddle. "When will she be home? I'll stop later."

Mrs. Randall straightened the collar on her dress and fidgeted with her necklace. She jutted her chin and tilted her head slightly. A smirk grew on her lips. "I'm afraid that will be impossible."

"Why? She's in good health, isn't she?"

"Oh my yes. The best actually. You see, shortly after you left Mr. Clayton came round courting."

"But isn't he already married?" Mayme cleared her throat and blinked rapidly as she tried to understand.

"He was, yes. But sadly his wife recently died in childbirth. He needed someone to help him with the baby. It was a quick courtship."

No, no, no. Mayme raised her hat above her head and carved her hand through her hair. She held it back for a moment before releasing it and replacing her hat.

"I just can't believe this." The Iris she knew wouldn't have gone willingly into that arrangement.

"Well, you should. They're very happy. And, honestly, it was time. I might even become a grandmother in the spring."

"Did you talk her into that?"

Mrs. Randall snorted. "As I told you in the past, every woman needs a man to look out for her. Iris is in her prime. Now, I think it's best you'd be going. I'll give her your regards when I see her."

Mayme's stomach clenched. *I just can't believe this. Iris wasn't ready to get married, let alone have a baby.* Something told her Mrs. Randall had something like this planned all along and had apparently just bided her time until the opportunity arose. She'd known her daughter would seek Mayme's advice so it had to be done while Mayme was on her run.

The entire scenario made Mayme angry and sad at the same time. She didn't bother to say goodbye to Mrs. Randall. The point had been made. Because of her choices, Mayme wasn't welcome anymore.

Mayme dug her heels into Duster's side and cantered away from the house, although she had to pull her up quickly because of the rutted road.

She felt empty, like she'd lost a friend. In a way she did, because in all likelihood, Mrs. Randall would never give up Iris's whereabouts let alone allow her to visit.

Mr. Smart waved to her as she passed the mercantile. He still hadn't hired her replacement so drove Ox into town every morning before dawn to prepare for the day. She wondered briefly if he was waiting for her to tire of the post rider work and come back to work for him. Maybe someday, she thought. But right now she felt a need to get back on the trail again. If she stayed in Eagle Rock, there'd be a good chance she'd go searching for Iris and undoubtedly have a confrontation with Mrs. Randall; One that could up nasty and dissolving any hopes of ever seeing Iris again.

LAWRENCE REMOVED HIS spectacles and rubbed the bridge of his nose. "So sad. Mr. Prescott was one of our best riders." He unrolled a parchment map on the desk, put his glasses back on and studied it.

Mayme watched as he traced her route with his finger and then that of what was Billy's. He scratched his balding head and sighed.

"I have a proposition for you, Nathan. How would you feel about running both routes? It will put you out on the trail for longer, but I am willing to offer you double what you're paid now and an extra one-percent for your troubles."

"So you'd be basically be giving me Billy's wage."

"If you wish to put it that way, yes, plus the one percent."

Mayme turned and looked out the doorway. She was flattered Lawrence thought she could handle both routes. The pay would be right enough that in less than two years' time she could buy her own land. That in and of itself was very attractive. But she couldn't ignore the increased danger. After all, Billy had lost his life on that route. She weighed both options in her mind. She not only had to think about the danger, there was the additional miles she'd be asking Duster to carry her over to consider.

"I'll make a deal with you. I will take on the extra route for the time being. But if it proves too much, I will request that you find a replacement. I have to warn you though, with winter coming on that may be sooner than later. That said, I'll do my best."

"YOU'LL NEED TO take a pack horse, Mayme. There's no way you'll be able to carry enough supplies to live on in those mountains between deliveries." Mr. Smart drummed his fingers on the table while eating dinner. "I think you should take Billy's horse. Use him as a pack horse."

"Red?" Mayme shook her head. "He's a pain in the behind."

"I'd give you Ox, but he's too old. And Sage is too unreliable." Mr. Smart rose from his chair and picked up their empty plates.

Dinner had consisted of rabbit stew with loads of potatoes and carrots added to the congealed gravy. Combined with the thick slab of buttered bread, Mayme was full to bursting.

"Since I can't afford another horse yet, I'll take Red on loan from you." Mayme couldn't see she had much of a choice at the moment.

"Fair enough. Keep in mind too that Red is familiar with that route."

"I hadn't thought of that."

Mr. Smart put the plates in the sink and disappeared into another room. He returned with a pistol.

"I want you to take this with you. It's a Colt revolver. It takes the same bullets as your Winchester. Use it for close targets. By that I mean no farther away than sixty feet. You can use the rifle beyond that distance."

Mayme knew without a doubt he was referring to Indians. She hefted the pistol. The grip fit well in her hand and seemed balanced.

"We'll shoot a few rounds tomorrow morning before you leave."

WHEN MAYME RODE out of town the next morning, she found more room in the saddle. The only thing, other than herself, that Duster carried was the saddle and mochila. Red carried food and clothing for Mayme and oats for both horses. The extra weight seemed to settle Red and make him focus on the business at hand.

Mr. Smart had made her promise that should Indians give her chase, she would drop Red's line and let Duster run for her life. She hated the thought of letting them have Red in favor of escape, but if it became a life or death situation, she'd have to do it. It was highly unlikely the Indians would harm Red. The tribes in these mountains were well-versed horse-keepers. The Indians valued horses as much as the white man coveted gold.

Chapter Nineteen

HOUR BY HOUR the cloud deck grew lower, thicker, and darker. Mayme had already put an extra layer on an hour ago. She reined Duster to a stop, got down and pulled her coat out of the pack Red carried. She tugged it up her arms, pulled it over her shoulders, and tightened the collar around her neck.

Before the approaching storm there'd been clear sky, sun falling upon new-fallen snow. A soft breeze had blown from the west. It was moist not cold. The trees had been stripped of their white covering of frost by the recent wind. There was a mutter of thunder rumbling in the distance.

She'd been delivering mail on both routes for close to a month and a half. With each passing day, more evidence of the approaching winter made itself known. The days were getting shorter and because of that she'd had to make camp earlier. She'd taken to erecting a small canvas lean-to at night to capture the heat and protect her from the rain. But this morning she had woken to a two-inch covering of snow. Breakfast had been a couple of cold strips of jerky on the trail because the snow had completely extinguished the fire. The small pile of firewood was wet and useless. It was futile to start a fire from scratch only to have to put it out again shortly thereafter.

After wiping the snow off the backs of the horses with a piece of burlap, she'd tacked them up and headed out. The new snow had made the ground slippery in some downhill spots. Duster handled it well. Red was another story. Ever since his rescue, he'd bonded tightly with Duster to the point of having to be literally touching her whenever he became a little unsure of himself. Mayme tried to correct him by shouting "whoa" whenever he tried to push past, and even sometimes had to kick him in the chest with her heel to help him regain his senses. She'd told Duster several times to kick him, but to no avail.

On one hand, Red's insecurity made her furious because it made him extremely pushy. But when he wasn't being ponied, he was quite affectionate to the point of nickering every time she walked away from the horses. The guilt she developed made her quickly forgive him for his daily offenses. He'd been through a lot. And honestly, who knew what he'd seen when Billy was killed? More often than not, she'd turn around and give him some extra scratches under his chin. Even though he was a pain sometimes, Mayme found she was growing as attached to Red as she was to Duster.

Fortunately, the route here on out to Orofino Creek was relatively easy. There were no narrow trails along steep drop-offs, only mostly uninterrupted forest with a gentle incline. Mayme was looking forward to ending the day with less irritation of Red.

Whenever she could find a gap in the tree canopy Mayme looked skyward and checked the encroaching storm. After a few short hours, it was nearly upon her. And it wasn't pretty. She looked around for a place to hunker down and keep warm and dry. But unlike in the higher altitudes, there were no rock outcroppings.

A group of close growing pines caught her eye. They were barely taller than the horses and small in diameter, but if she worked fast, she could somehow drape the canvas over them so that the horses could have some protection as well.

Suddenly the clouds darkened the sun and sky. The north wind struck with a frigidness she'd never felt before. The air was thick with furious snow. She dug her heels into Duster's side and pointed her toward the trees. There was a hard tug on the saddle horn as the slack was tugged out from Red's rope. He caught up quickly.

"Come on!" Mayme clucked to both horses. Whether they could hear her or not was anybody's guess, but something got them moving. Maybe it was the desperation in her voice, or maybe they were as troubled as she was.

The horses rushed into the trees and disturbed the snow that'd already collected on the branches. It slid onto the saddle and into her lap. She brushed it off and instantly regretted it. The snow clung to her exposed hands. They ached with the cold. She wiped them under her armpits as best she could, but it did nothing to warm them up.

The cold had crept into her boots while she was riding. She'd managed to keep it mostly at bay by alternately standing up in the stirrups and sitting down. Although she could still feel her toes, they were getting increasingly stiff to move.

Mayme swung her leg over the saddle and slid down Duster's side. She tried to ignore the stabbing pain as her feet hit the ground, but in a way felt grateful she could still feel something. She clenched her chattering teeth to keep them from breaking. She blew into her hands and rubbed them together. Her deerskin gloves were buried somewhere at the bottom of the pack and not easily accessible. She damned herself for not getting them out this morning before she left camp.

The horses exhaled thick white plumes that were at once swept away by the wind. Frosty icicles hung from their whiskers. Both shook their heads to rid themselves of the snow caking on their faces.

The wind blew relentlessly through the trees. Its howl was the only thing Mayme heard. It would be futile to try and put the canvas over the horses. It would only blow away. She pulled Red up alongside Duster and then stood in the middle of them to block the wind. Her face stung from the cold and the force of the snow hitting her. The flakes weren't soft and moist like last night, but crystals of ice mixed with dry snow.

Mayme crossed her arms over her chest and lowered her chin to keep any heat from escaping the neck of her coat. *I've got to stay warm.* She alternated her weight from one leg to another to try and force warm blood into her feet. Her jaw hurt from trying to keep her teeth together. She'd never been so cold in her life.

The tempest continued for hours, piling up snow in drifts and blinding what was left of the day with ice-white dust. As Mayme got colder, she bent over against the cold and protected her eyes with her arms. Trees loomed into her vision and then vanished, swallowed in white.

At one point Mayme tried shoving her frozen hands between the saddle blanket and Duster's back. Blood circulation and feeling slowly crept back into her digits. She nearly cried with the pain.

Standing between the horses was no longer helping to keep warm. When she could finally move her fingers she pounded the ice-crusted buckle of the horse-pack with her fist. It finally relented and she pushed the stiff leather through the buckle. It took her four tries before she could make her fingers work again to grasp and pull out the bedroll and canvas.

If I don't get warm, I'm going to die. She'd have to leave the horses to fend for themselves against the storm. They showed no sign of wanting to leave the minimal shelter they'd been standing in for hours. She only hoped Duster's loyalty would keep her close. She knew Red wouldn't stray far from Duster.

The impenetrable thicket of trees behind her was her only hope of survival. She dropped to her knees and crawled in as far as could. Every movement was an effort. Through a series of moving back and forth she managed to roll herself up in the blanket with the canvas draped lopsidedly over her.

Mayme knew shivering was her body's attempt to get warm. Being out of the wind helped slightly. But she was still cold. Very cold. She started to get sleepy and knew right then that she was in trouble. Despite fighting it as best she could, her heavy eyelids drooped and closed. The only relief she got was that the shivering had stopped and her muscles relaxed. She sighed deeply and drifted off.

MAYME SLOWLY REGAINED consciousness. She opened her eyes, but all she could see was blackness. Her arms and legs seemed tightly bound, but she recalled rolling herself up into the blanket and canvas. *That's probably why I can't move. Too tired.*

A horse snorted from nearby and she registered a flicker of relief. Duster, and therefore Red, were close by. The wind had quieted. Instead of the raging noise, a muffled breeze sang through the canopy.

As she became more aware, she realized her head was on an incline from her feet. And she felt movement. And muffled voices. Someone had come along and saved her. Tears welled up behind her eyelids. She never thought she'd wake up again when she had closed her eyes.

"Hello!" She tried in vain to wiggle enough to catch her savior's attention. "Thank God you found me. Would you please tell me who you are?"

The movement stopped and she heard another voice. Two? Were there two people out there? She wished she could understand what they were saying.

"Would you help me out of this?" Mayme wiggled as hard as she could, but to no avail. A sudden jerk backward and the movement began again. She struggled against the tight binding but still couldn't loosen it. After a while, she was just too tuckered out to try anymore. Her weariness and the warmth eventually lulled her to sleep.

Mayme had no idea how long she'd slept. It could've been minutes or hours. She just couldn't be sure. Although any movement was severely limited, she remained warm and comfortable. There was no point in staring at the darkness, so she closed her eyes.

Time was countless while traveling in the cocoon. Mayme lost track of how many times she dozed off. She had no idea if it was day or night, only that she was alive, warm, and not alone. But she was confused as to who would've come across her in the storm. Had they sent someone out to search for her like she'd had to do for Billy? But she hadn't been overdue in Oro Fino Creek when the storm hit. Who was it then? Her mind raced as she searched for answers to unresolved questions.

Mayme felt something slide under her back and butt. She was abruptly flipped over and off whatever she'd been laying on. She landed hard with a grunt. There was a chorus of muffled voices. And laughter. Somebody was laughing that she got tossed off?

"Hey! What's the big idea? That was kind of harsh." Mayme rolled from side to side and felt a slight give as she moved onto her left side. She continued unrolling until finally her arm was free enough to pull the cover off her face.

More laughter.

The bright sunlight reflecting off the snow blinded her. Tears formed and blurred her vision. She shaded her eyes with her arm and blinked until they slowly adjusted. Everything eventually came into focus as she wiped the tears out of her eyes.

At least ten shadowy figures stood in a circle around her. She couldn't make out any faces because of the intense sunshine backlighting everything. There were various mumblings and more laughter. But it was in a language she didn't recognize.

Suddenly she knew. She hadn't been saved by a search party or good Samaritans. Rather, she'd been captured by Indians. She shoved her fist into her mouth to hold back a scream. Her heart raced to the point of exploding. *God, no. Please don't let it be so. There has to be some kind of mistake.*

Mayme's first instinct was to jump to her feet and flee. But she knew it would be of no use. In her condition, she'd never get away. More than likely she would fall from a well-placed arrow in her spine. She couldn't trust her legs would obey her. They were shaky at best. She felt weak. Her bladder loosened. She took a shuddering breath and worked to keep from wetting herself.

"Mogo'ne."

Mayme turned her head toward the voice. A series of high clouds had floated in, giving her eyes a break and allowing her to see more clearly. Like the rest of her onlookers, the warrior was very dark complected. A thick braid of black hair dangled over both shoulders. The ends were wrapped in fur. Even in the cold he wore only a loincloth.

"Nana." One of the others pointed at Mayme's chest.

"Mogo'ne." The first Indian grabbed his crotch, jiggled it, and shook his head. This caused another round of laughter.

"Ponzo-bert!"

A woman tentatively shouldered her way through. She wore a fringed deerskin dress brightly decorated with beads and porcupine quills. Unlike Mayme's captor, her thick black hair flowed freely over her shoulders. She kept her eyes downcast as if in humiliation.

The warrior who had called for her pointed at Mayme. "O-yem-fat-sup."

The woman nodded and gruffly pulled Mayme to her feet.

Mayme's head swam and her knees threatened to buckle. She tried to mask her fear with aggressiveness. She yanked her arm out of the woman's grasp. A large arm snaked itself around her middle and picked her up. She tried to turn in his stronghold and only managed to get a glimpse of the amused smile the warrior wore.

"Nuikwi."

The warrior carried her behind the woman who was walking toward a tepee. The woman pulled the flap aside and went inside. The warrior dropped Mayme at the entrance and she went to her knees. He grabbed her by the collar of her coat and tossed her inside.

Mayme landed in a heap next to a low-burning fire. Sparks rose from a displaced rock she'd pushed into the embers when she went down. She quickly rolled away from it and came face to face with a young girl. She was thin, and had vivid dark eyes over high cheekbones. She looked at Mayme with a blended mixture of fright, mockery, impatience, and scorn. Her dress was adorned with woven horsehair sewed in a pattern resembling the wind.

"Anta." The girl pointed at Mayme and giggled.

"Ba'nangu." The woman called Ponzo-bert ignored the girl and motioned for Mayme to stand.

Mayme pushed up on shaky legs. She closed her eyes for a few seconds to combat the dizziness and nausea. She opened them and saw an ancient woman sitting in the shadows on the other side of the fire. The flames cast eerie shadows across her wrinkled face. She opened her mouth in a toothless grin and then shoved what looked like a strap of nameless dried meat into her mouth.

Mayme's attention was forced back to Ponzo-bert as she felt a hard tug on the front of her coat.

"Ca-tto'aih." Ponzo-bert held her palms upward and flicked her fingers up and down.

"You want me to take my coat off?"

There wasn't even a hint of understanding on the woman's face. Mayme raised her eyebrows and unbuttoned the top button of her coat.

Ponzo-bert nodded.

Mayme undid the front of her coat and then slipped it off. The interior of the tepee was warm enough to comfortably have it off. The scent of smoky pinesap hung in the air.

"Ca-tto'aih." Ponzo-bert repeated her hand motions.

Mayme thought she understood now. For some reason the woman wanted her to take her tops off. She pulled both shirts off in one motion and stood with nothing on except for her chest wrap.

Suddenly the flap of the tepee was thrown aside and the warrior stomped in holding a large knife in his hand. He glared at Mayme as he strode to her in two long strides.

"O-yem-fat-sup."

Mayme didn't move, and he grabbed the front of her wrapping in one fist and cleanly sliced through it with the knife. The material fell away to her feet, and Mayme instinctively crossed her arms over her chest.

The warrior threw his head back, laughed, and pointed at Mayme's breasts. "Bizi." He promptly turned around and strode out of the tepee.

Mayme swallowed audibly. Something brushed her arm. She turned and found Ponzo-bert holding her shirts.

Ponzo-bert nodded. "Ca'iju."

Mayme heard more laughter outside as she slipped her shirts over her head. It seemed that they had wanted to find out if she was a girl or a boy. Hopefully being a girl would keep her safe. She most certainly didn't want to have the same demise as Billy.

Even though she had no idea of what her fate might be, an unexpected release of tension allowed her to breathe freer. She pressed a palm to her heart and closed her eyes for a moment.

A dog barked outside the tepee and she heard horses neighing in the distance. A pang of guilt brought a tear to her eye. She'd completely forgotten about Duster and Red. Where were they? Did her captors bring them along? Or were they left to fend for themselves in the frigid mountains. She had to find out.

Mayme took a step toward the door. But the Indian woman grabbed her coat collar.

"Osh-Tisch!"

The warrior flung the entrance flap open and stormed inside. He glared at Mayme, sending her heart racing once again. But this time, instead of a knife, he held a length of rope in his hand. He knotted the ends around each ankle, allowing a short bit in between which would allow her to take short steps. If she had any thoughts of running away, they'd been sufficiently dashed.

Osh-Tisch stood to his full height in front of her. The look in his eyes dared her to try something, anything. She averted her eyes in submission. He grunted and walked out; apparently satisfied he had deterred any escape.

"Yetwitigi."

Mayme shook her head. "I don't understand." She showed her palms and shrugged.

"Yetwitigi." The young girl patted the buffalo robe she was sitting on. "Yetwitigi."

Mayme shuffled, because that was all she could do, over next to the girl. She crouched down, braced herself with her hands, and sat down clumsily.

The girl nodded and turned her attention to the hide in her lap. It was tan colored and looked to be very supple and soft. She used a short knife to cut fringe.

Mayme made note of the knife. She might have an opportunity to use it to cut off her bindings.

As if reading her thoughts, the girl looked her in the eyes, shook her head, and made a cutting motion across her neck.

There was no misunderstanding the meaning. Mayme would be killed if she attempted an escape.

"Tekkahpaitseh." Ponzo-bert offered her a strap of meat. "Natekkat-i."

Mayme looked at the young girl who made a chewing motion and rubbed her belly. It seemed they were trying to tell her the meat was good. She took the proffered meat and put an end in her mouth. She instantly recognized the flavour as venison. Her mouth watered in response and she wondered how long it'd been since she'd last eaten. Time had slipped away in the storm. She had no memory between the time she fell asleep in the snow and when she had awoken and discovered she'd been found.

They said no more to her for the duration of the day. Mayme was surprised to see darkness beyond the tepee flap when Osh-Tisch returned. She'd lost all sense of time.

Osh-Tisch avoided looking at her at all. As far as Mayme was concerned, she wasn't there at all.

Ponzo-bert prepared four bowls of food, handing one each to the girl, old woman, and Osh-Tisch before sitting next to him. They all ignored her while they ate.

Mayme stole glances at them. Her stomach demanded more than the small strap of meat she'd been given earlier. But nothing else was offered.

Later, the women started arranging the buffalo hides in preparation for sleeping. Osh-Tisch took Mayme by the arm and pulled her up. He pointed to the flap. She made the mistake of hesitating. He shoved her gruffly toward the opening. The slack between her ankles disappeared and she nearly fell face forward. He made no move to help her.

Once outside, Osh-Tisch led her to the far side of the village. She felt sick with fear. Was this it then? Her time to die? Had he decided she wasn't valuable enough? Goose bumps peppered her flesh and her teeth chattered. She regretted not grabbing her coat on the way out. But if he was going to kill her, what did it matter?

He tugged her to a stop next to a tree. As he stared hard into her eyes, he moved his loincloth to the side and urinated in the snow. He finished and jutted his chin toward her. "Naadoihu." He pointed at the yellow snow and then her.

Mayme had had to pee for hours, but she wasn't keen on doing it in front of a man, let alone this one. Although she couldn't see she had much of a choice. But she sure wasn't going to bare her bum to him. She unbuttoned her trousers and slid them down as she crouched. She nearly wept with relief as her urine began to flow.

Osh-Tisch pushed her back into the tepee, and she was immediately grateful for the warmth that washed over her. To her surprise, the tepee was much warmer than Mr. Smart's house even with a fire blazing all night long. Of course it was smaller, but there'd been mornings when she'd seen her breath when she woke.

"Ah-be-guy." Osh-Tisch pointed to the buffalo hide on the opposite side of the opening. He got down on his knees, glanced at Ponzo-bert, laid down, and pulled a hide over him.

Mayme felt all eyes on her as she carefully made her way over. She was terrified of falling into the fire. She doubted anyone would help her.

She sat down on the hide and stretched her legs in front of her.

"Tukkwan." Ponzo-bert lifted a side of the hide Mayme sat on and indicated with a horizontal chopping motion that she should lay between both hides.

Mayme averted her eyes and smiled graciously. Once she adjusted her bound legs beneath the hide and convinced herself she wouldn't be killed in the night, she took a deep breath and relaxed. It wasn't long before she heard the deep breathing of sleep from the others.

In the dim light, she took advantage of being the only one awake. She'd kept her gaze downward to show submission for the majority of the time she'd been in the tepee. Up until now, she'd not had an opportunity to take a good look around.

The round-shaped tepee was very spacious with an open area a little off-centered at the top to let the smoke out. The majority of the floor was covered with buffalo hides, but there were also deer, sheep, and elk skins.

Pouches made of buffalo hide hung from the poles. The few times Mayme had dared to glance up, she'd seen Ponzobert and the girl get tools, leggings, and several handfuls of what looked like dried berries from the various pouches. The straps of meat had been retrieved from the birch bark boxes on the floor beneath the bags. An elaborately painted warrior's shield, a lance, and bow and arrows hung to the right of it all, and directly above where Osh-Tisch now slept. A fur bag and another very small pouch were suspended near his head. The tepee was nicely and efficiently laid out. The absence of furniture did nothing to detract from the hominess.

Osh-Tisch snorted in his sleep. Mayme watched to see if he was going to wake up and catch her looking around. Now that he had sufficiently warned, more like intimidated, her about the consequences should she attempt an escape, she came to the conclusion that she'd have to abide by their rules and lifestyle until such time she was rescued. Until then, she reasoned, she'd have to pretend she was staying with strangers. Except for her legs being tied. She hoped that wouldn't last long.

Chapter Twenty

MAYME WOKE WHEN she sensed more than heard movement. Osh-Tisch was up and gone. Ponzo-bert and the girl were busy preparing the morning meal.

She raised her head slightly and met the eyes of the old woman who watched her intently.

"Wemmiha." The old woman closed her eyes for a moment. She opened them and revealed her bare gums in a smile.

"Tekkahpaitseh." Ponzo-bert held out a small wooden bowl. She made a bowl-to-mouth motion.

Mayme sat up and took it. The smell emanating from it made her mouth water. Her stomach growled in anticipation of getting more than a strap of meat. Hunks of meat sat suspended in thin gravy with gooseberries and acorns. She raised the bowl to her lips and sipped. It was delicious. She drained the liquid and picked the solids out with her fingers.

"Caan-kammah." The old woman smiled and rubbed her belly.

"Can-kammeh." Mayme did her best to imitate her, but knew she had stumbled terribly.

"Caan-kammeh."

"Caan-kammeh." Mayme smiled brightly at the enthusiastic nods from all three women. She had a good idea the phrase meant "tastes good," and the fact that she had tried to say it pleased them.

There was very little talking between the women after that. It seemed they were all engrossed in their own chores. After a quick trip to the urine tree, during which she was accompanied by Ponzo-bert, Mayme watched with growing interest from her sleeping place. The young girl brought out her sewing and the old woman dozed on and off. It seemed Ponzo-bert was in charge of all the activities within the tepee.

Although Mayme couldn't understand the language, every time Ponzo-bert said something, the girl jumped up and did what she was ordered to do.

When the sun was directly overhead, sending rays streaking down the smoke hole, there was a scratching sound on the tepee from the outside.

"Osh-Tisch tsategi-nei' aiwa tu hudda," a voice said.

Ponzo-bert and the girl quickly put on vests made of wolf fur. The old woman nudged Mayme with her foot. "Namasuah." She pointed at Mayme's coat.

Mayme rose to her feet and put it on. She glanced at the old woman who nodded.

"Wookahtea." The girl removed a knife from one of the pouches and motioned for Mayme to follow her out.

Mayme shaded her eyes against the reflection of the sun on the snow. The air was crisp and clean. Bare patches of dirt where the snow had melted were rimmed with ice. Several youngsters, dressed in deer hide garments and rabbit skin vests, played an Indian version of hopscotch as they leaped from one to the other. Their elaborately beaded moccasins reached nearly to their knees.

Ponzo-bert led them to a small group of women. All of them held knives and were speaking with great animation. Mayme looked in the direction they faced and saw the reason for their excitement. Osh-Tisch and three others approached on horseback. Each man led a horse with a large deer lashed over its back.

The women followed the successful hunters into the circle of tepees and converged onto the deer as they came to a halt. The men dismounted and after the deer were taken off the horses, led them away.

Her presence momentarily forgotten, Mayme watched with fascination as the women expertly and efficiently skinned and butchered each animal. Soon large chunks of meat roasted in the main fire pit. Other straps of meat were hung from poles above smaller fires.

Mayme felt a sharp tug on her arm. The young girl from

Osh-Tisch's tepee stood next to her, holding one of the deer hides.

She pointed at Mayme. "Teteaiwoppih."

Mayme nodded. She had no idea what she was agreeing to, but knew it was the correct action because the girl grinned and quickly walked away. She tried to keep up with the girl's pace, but the tether around her ankles hindered her greatly.

The girl swivelled her head around to make sure Mayme was following. She rolled her eyes, frowned, and stomped back to Mayme. The girl bent down in front of Mayme and with a quick flick of her knife, cut the rope.

"Teteaiwoppih," she said more urgently and trotted away.

With her feet now free, Mayme was able to easily keep up with the girl. She wondered what Osh-Tisch would think of the girl freeing her. With nearly everybody occupied with the butchering, she could handily make a run for it. But the grisly scene of Billy's body popped into her head and she decided against it for the time being.

The girl led Mayme to a large log that had been propped up on one end by another shorter log. Two rocks were wedged in on either side to prevent it from rolling off. The bark had been scraped off, leaving a smooth surface upon which the girl straddled. She draped the hide over the edge and removed the knife from a sheath tied around her leg. She looked at Mayme expectantly.

Mayme shrugged and got a frown in return.

"I'm sorry. I don't understand what you want."

The girl sheathed the knife and slid off the log. She took Mayme by the arm and guided her to the tip of the log. There, she picked up the edge of the hide and put it in Mayme's right hand. The girl then moved to Mayme's left and handed her another part so that Mayme's hands were spaced three feet away from the other.

Mayme had to clench her hand tightly over the slimy hide to hold it. There were still chunks of meat, fat and silver skin clinging it. A gaping hole indicated where the arrow had pierced and brought the animal down.

The girl took her seat and put her hands over Mayme's and squeezed slightly. "Himakka."

Mayme thought she understood the girl's directive; hold the end of the hide while she did whatever she was going to do with it, which quickly became clear.

The girl pulled on the hide and stretched it over the wood between them. By expertly using the knife, she scraped the hide clean without putting a nick in it. Two brindled, well-muscled dogs crept in and alternately grabbed the scraps.

"What's your name?" Mayme knew the girl didn't have a clue what she just said, but she felt the need to talk anyway.

The girl paused and furrowed her brows. She looked at Mayme curiously and shook her head.

"My name is Mayme, but have been going by Nathan ever since I've been riding for the post. I'm supposed to be a boy. But I guess you all have figured that out." She couldn't help but giggle quietly. "I guess it doesn't matter what I am now."

The Indian girl set the knife on the hide and wiped her hands on the fur. She captured Mayme's gaze and patted her chest with her palm. "Muha ai-wa." She tapped her chest again. "Muha ai-wa."

"Is that your name?" Mayme tapped her own chest. "Mayme."

The girl pointed at Mayme and carefully said, "Ma-eem." She tapped her chest again. "Muha ai-wa."

Mayme licked her lips and cleared her throat. It was difficult for her to hear where they accented their words. It was a very nasal language with intermittent clicks. "Mwa-a-wa." She patted her chest again and repeated her name.

The girl smiled. She pointed to herself. "Muha ai-wa." And then to Mayme. "Ma-eem."

"Yes!" Mayme finally felt like she was getting somewhere. She pointed at the knife. "Knife."

Muha ai-wa picked the knife up and looked at Mayme. "We-its."

"We-its."

Muha ai-wa smiled brightly.

"We-its. Knife."

"We-its. Neef."

MAYME AND MUHA AI-WA continued to "talk" for the remainder of the afternoon. Mayme helped Muha ai-wa stretch the hide tight and tie it on a frame to dry. Afterward, they helped Ponzo-bert cut strips of meat from a hindquarter and hang them to make jerky. They traded the knife back and forth as they tested words and associations. Even Ponzo-bert chuckled a couple times at their silliness. They returned to the tepee and got the old woman laughing outright. She slapped her thighs and clapped as she listened. Their frivolousness was cut short as Osh-Tisch returned to the tepee. But even then, Mayme and Muha ai-wa traded grins when they thought he wasn't looking.

If Osh-Tisch noticed the tether binding Mayme's legs together had been cut, he showed no sign of it or being displeased. Nevertheless, Mayme took small steps so it wouldn't be blatantly obvious. Osh-Tisch paid her no attention. After a huge meal of venison roast, he sat cross-legged and smoked a pipe filled with sweet grass. The pipe went out, and he tapped the ashes into the fire, crawled between the buffalo hides, and was soon fast asleep.

MAYME AND MUHA AI-WA were virtually inseparable from that point on. It seemed the rest of the tribe, who Mayme found out were Shoshone Indians, approved of their growing friendship as well as Mayme's valiant attempt to learn their language. She found more times than not, she was able to understand what they were trying to convey. And if she couldn't, most of the tribes-people showed much patience in helping her. But only the women spoke to her. None of the men said anything to her, let alone show any acknowledgement of her. She found she didn't mind. She wanted to avoid making any of the men angry for fear of her life. Although she wasn't so sure her life was as expendable now as it might have been when she was first captured.

The Shoshone people didn't have a complicated language because the vocabulary was limited to a few hundred words. However it took practice remembering where the stops and nasal inclinations were. Mayme spent hours imitating Muha ai-wa. Muha ai-wa, on the other hand picked up the general English words very quickly.

Time flew by quickly for Mayme. Her days were filled with helping Muha ai-wa and Ponzo-bert with daily chores, including cooking and sewing. As the days grew longer and the snow melted and came less frequently, the women of the tribe wandered farther afield to gather the lush green sprouts of wild onion and the sweet flowered fireweed. Wild strawberries and grapes grew in the meadows. Cattails lined marshes and small ponds.

Mayme was amazed at the plants the Shoshone utilized. One day the entire force of women descended upon the low-lying shaded areas in search of wild ginger. Muha ai-wa explained that it was an important medicinal staple. The dried roots were used to reduce fever and the fresh ones were bound together to stop bleeding and promote healing. Mayme lived in fascination as every day she learned something new.

Chapter Twenty-one

"REMEMBER WHEN OSH-TISCH brought me to the village?" Mayme asked Muha ai-wa one summer morning. They'd been able to shed their fur vests in favour of short-sleeved deerskin shirts. Mayme's cotton clothing had finally succumbed to wear. Ponzo-bert and Muha ai-wa had surprised her one morning by presenting her with attire made entirely of tanned deer hide. Mayme spent evenings sewing beads onto it by firelight.

"Hadug. I mean, yes." Muha ai-wa smiled at her quick translation. She stepped forward into the mud and with a skillful flick of her knife, decapitated a cattail flower from its spike.

Mayme took the cigar-looking blossom from her and dropped it into a pouch. Baked over a slow fire, they'd be eating them like corn-on-the-cob tonight. Ponzo-bert would pound some into a yellow-colored flour for biscuits at a later date. "Would I have been killed if I'd been a boy?"

"No." Sticky mud squished beneath Muha ai-wa's moccasins. Her feet sank a few inches deeper.

"Careful." Mayme held the pouch open for three more flower heads. "Then why was it so important to find out?"

"Because Osh-Tisch wanted to know if you would be my companion or my husband."

"Oh." Mayme was confused. "The Shoshone are friendly with the white man? Um. Taipo?"

"Yes. Ponzo-bert was returned to our tribe by two taipos. She had been kidnapped many years ago by the Hidatsas tribe. We will forever be indebted to the taipos."

They worked in silence for a while. Mayme was trying to make sense of what she'd been made to believe by the people in Oro Fino Creek and Eagle Rock. She'd learned that the Shoshone were not the blood-thirsty savages everybody thought them to be. In fact, she'd only known them to be a peaceful tribe. During the many months she'd lived with Osh-Tisch's tribe, she'd only seen the men leave in hunting groups. She'd never seen a raiding or war party.

"Will you stay with the Shoshone?" Muha ai-wa broke into Mayme's thoughts. She stood in mud nearly to her knees. Yellow cattail pollen covered her arms and parts of her face like a mask.

Mayme's almost laughed at the sight before her until Muha ai-wa's question sank in.

"What do you mean? I don't see as I have much of a choice. I can't imagine Osh-Tisch would ever allow me to leave."

Muha ai-wa shrugged and resumed harvesting cattails.

After a while, with two pouches full of cattails and a smaller one packed tight with serviceberries and field mint, they decided to follow the stream back to the village. In addition to washing off the mud from the marsh, they hoped to find some crawfish hiding under rocks.

Although the day was quite warm, the rushing channel still showed remnants of the snowmelt high in the mountains. The water was silt gray and ice cold. White birch and cottonwoods grew a safe distance from the water's edge. Several ragged stumps and overturned trees were evidence of the ones that had succumbed to the raging spring floods. The force of the water had sheered everything in its path, leaving nothing but a nice silty area for grass to grow.

Muha ai-wa removed her moccasins and leggings and dropped them on the ground next to Mayme who was content to sit in the sun and rest. Although she had become quite fit in their meanderings afoot, Muha ai-wa had amazing stamina and could still run her ragged.

Mayme watched as Muha ai-wa took a tentative step into the water. And then another. She turned her head to look back at Mayme and playfully raised her eyebrows. Suddenly her feet went out from under her. With a sharp cry she went under and was quickly swept downstream.

"Muha ai-wa!" Mayme jumped to her feet and raced after her. The water was moving too fast. She saw the panic and fear on Muha ai-wa's face. Her head bobbed above the water. And then she was gone.

Mayme ran hard until she finally had to stop, bend over, and gulp air. Sweat mixed with tears and snaked down her face. The blood pounded so loudly in her ears she couldn't hear the roar of the water. She had to find her! Mayme filled her lungs with air and pushed on.

She nearly cried in frustration as she came upon a huge jam of wash and overturned trees as tall as she was piled in her path. The rushing water had forced tons of debris up onto the sharp bend. The undergrowth was too thick to go around it. She'd have to climb over.

It took nearly all of her strength to pull herself up and over the entwined pile of massive logs. Branches stuck out in every direction. Sand and pebbles filled some of the spaces, but they were precarious at best. As she stepped on them, her foot broke through, jolting every joint in her body.

Mayme finally got to the other side. She sported several scrapes and a slightly strained ankle. She felt bruised everywhere. Small prickles of blood and raised flesh peppered her arms from the unrelenting brambles. Wild rose had taken up residence on the other side and the thorns were relentless in their quest to hang onto clothes and skin. She gritted her teeth and pushed through, crying out in determination and pain.

She ignored the burn in her legs and lungs as she ran. She had to keep going.

Mayme focused on the ground. It wouldn't do Muha ai-wa any good if she broke her leg while trying to find her.

She flung her leg over another log to get over it. And saw Muha ai-wa's body. The water had deposited the lifeless form on a sandbar in the middle of where the creek had widened out.

"Oh no. Please, no." Mayme hurried into the water. Although it was much shallower, the water still reached to the middle of her calves. She kept her eyes on Muha ai-wa and avoided looking at the running water. Her heart flew into her throat when she tripped over a submerged rock. Somehow she was able to regain her footing and balance.

"Muha ai-wa!" Mayme struggled to run the remaining distance. She fell to her knees as she reached her. She worked to catch her breath. Exhaustion made her hands shake as she reached for Muha ai-wa. Mayme sent a silent prayer to all the gods that she was still alive. She grasped her by the shoulder and tried to flip her onto her back. But her arms lacked the strength and she only succeeded in getting Muha ai-wa's halfway over. She rested on her side against Mayme's hip. Muha ai-wa's eyes were rolled back into her head. There was no rise and fall of her chest. Mayme leaned over and tried to hear a heartbeat. In doing so, she inadvertently put pressure on Muha ai-wa's stomach just below her ribs.

Water suddenly gushed from Muha ai-wa's mouth and she gave a great gasp, followed by a gut-wrenching cough. She looked at Mayme and coughed again. Mayme helped her get to her knees and she bent over heaving in her search for air. Muha ai-wa vomited brown water for several minutes. She hacked and spit to clear the remainder of the silty water from her stomach. Mayme rubbed Muha ai-wa's back, tears of relief streaming down her face.

Muha ai-wa's teeth chattered incessantly. Gooseflesh maintained a constant presence on Mayme's flesh too.

"We've got to get you warm. Can you walk?"

"Hadug."

Mayme helped her stand and draped Muha ai-wa's arm over her shoulder. "I've got you. Just hold on tight." Mayme wrapped an arm around her waist and pulled her close.

They waded slowly to the streambank. Mayme made sure each step was steady and solid to hold both of them. They reached the other side and took a rest in the remaining sunlight. Dusk wasn't that far off. There wasn't a cloud in the sky, indicative of an oncoming chilly night.

"Stay here. I'll get a fire going." Mayme rose unsteadily. She closed her eyes and let the relief of finding Muha ai-wa alive give her strength. Although she was bone tired, there was work to do.

Firewood was plentiful and Mayme didn't have to go too far to gather it. She had a crackling fire going in no time, thanks to the flint she and Muha ai-wa always carried.

They sat huddled next to the fire and warmth gradually reached the core of their bodies. Because of the breeze generated by the water, they wore their garments to dry, although Muha ai-wa only had on a deerskin shirt. Steam rose lazily from their bodies and was gently carried away. Neither said anything and eventually they both fell asleep with their heads resting on each other.

MAYME OPENED HER eyes the next morning and felt every bruise and ache from yesterday's event. She looked to Muha ai-wa, who was still sound asleep with her head resting on Mayme's shoulder.

Only ash and a few unburned end pieces of wood remained of the fire. But at least they were warm and dry again. Muha ai-wa's teeth no longer clacked together. Her body was still but for her breathing. The relentless shaking of her body to get warm had stopped.

Mayme stared into the remnants of the fire. It scared her to think how close she'd come to losing Muha ai-wa. She'd grown to love her as a sister. She felt that same familial affection toward Ponzo-bert as a mother, and the old woman, who she now knew as *Muha ada,* or Moon Raven, as a grandmother. Over the months, Osh-Tisch had become friendlier toward her. Although they rarely spoke, he treated her fairly and with kindness.

Muha ai-wa stirred and gradually woke. She sat up, rubbed her eyes, and looked around. "Before the sun set, I didn't think I would see another dawn."

Mayme hugged her close. "I didn't think you would either. You almost scared the life out of me."

Muha ai-wa's stomach growled.

"We should start walking. The pouches and your leggings and moccasins are a ways back."

The sun was hot and high in the sky again when they finally reached the spot where Muha ai-wa had been swept away. Along the way they ate whatever crickets and gooseberries they could find. But they still arrived hungry. Muha ai-wa shoved handfuls of berries and mint into her mouth and chewed while she dressed. Mayme rested on a log while she ate.

PONZO-BERT AND MUHA ada clucked disapprovingly as they arrived back at the village. Once Muha ai-wa relayed the story of how Mayme had rescued her and brought her back to life, Ponzo-bert set about preparing a hearty meal for them. She insisted they rest atop two buffalo hides placed on top of one another.

Osh-Tisch ate silently while Muha ai-wa retold the story. He flicked his eyes to Mayme. "Eshi eshi."

Mayme smiled and nodded. She knew it was a big deal for him to voice his thanks.

Mayme woke to an empty tepee the next morning. She was too comfortable to move, and if she didn't, she wouldn't be reminded of the beating her body had taken two days before. So she let her eyes drift to the blue sky through the hole at the top of the tepee. The poles seemed to point to the sky and she was reminded of what Muha ai-wa had taught her one snowy day when they chose to hide inside away from the frigid wind. *The tepee floor is the symbol of the earth, the walls a symbol of the sky, and the poles are links between the earth, man, and the spirit world in the sky.*

Mother would give birth to a cow if she saw me living here. It suddenly occurred to her that she hadn't thought about her parents in a very long time. Several full moons, in fact. She reminisced about Mr. Smart and Betty oftentimes but admittedly, although she felt bad that they undoubtedly thought her dead, she didn't miss them as much anymore.

She heard scratching outside the tepee just before the flap was flung aside.

"Are you going to sleep all day?" Muha ai-wa walked in and crossed her arms over her chest.

"I thought I might. You're a hard one to rescue." Mayme pushed herself up and stretched her back. She ran her fingers through hair that had grown past her shoulders. Later she'd divide it into two braids to keep cooler in the afternoon heat.

Mayme yawned. Muha ai-wa was obviously waiting for her. Besides, she had to pee anyway. She rose to her feet and stretched. She tested her ankle. Although it was still sore, she could bear weight on it. She followed Muha ai-wa out and kept her gaze to the ground while her eyes adjusted to the bright sun.

Giggling made Mayme look up. What appeared like the entire village stood in a semi-circle around Osh-Tisch's tepee. Every person wore a smile and she heard several call out, "Pop-pank."

Mayme looked at Muha ai-wa who stood next to Ponzo-bert. "What is going on?"

Several people moved to the side to make way for Osh-Tisch to walk through. He held a rifle, her rifle, in his hand.

Mayme took a step backward in confusion and felt her heels against the tepee.

Osh-Tisch stopped in front of her. Their eyes met and held. He finally broke the silence. "We have waited a long time for this moment. You will now forever be known as Pop-pank."

"It means jumping fish," Muha ai-wa whispered and grinned at her.

The villagers nodded and repeated her name. "Pop-pank."

"When I found you many moons ago, I took this from your saddle. I honor you by returning it." Osh-Tisch handed the gun to her.

Mayme looked at him in amazement.

"Yaakki." Osh-Tisch turned around and faced the direction he had come.

Once again, the people parted, but this time gave a wider path to a warrior who led Duster beside him. Duster pranced, shook her head, and snorted in defiance. She alternately pinned her ears and tried to grab his arm with her teeth.

Although Mayme had caught glimpses of Duster and Red from afar, she'd never been allowed to visit her horses. She assumed because they thought she might take that opportunity to escape. But here Duster was, saddled and bridled, and looking fat and sassy. She stood there with her mouth agape.

The warrior passed Duster's reins to Osh-Tisch and joined the crowd.

"This horse is also yours. I honor you by returning her. She is with foal."

Duster lunged and nipped Osh-Tisch on the shoulder. She walked forward and put her muzzle against Mayme's chest and nickered.

Tears streaked down Mayme's face. She wrapped her arms around Duster's neck and squeezed. She didn't dare ask about Red as it would be a sign of greed on her part.

"Osh-Tisch is pleased to be rid of her. She has bitten and kicked him more than once." Muha ai-wa came to Mayme's side.

"I don't know what to say."

"Osh-Tisch is giving you your freedom."

Mayme looked at Osh-Tisch and then back to Muha ai-wa. "You knew? That's why you asked me that question while we picked cattails."

"I only knew he would let you go. And I knew you would go."

"But—" Mayme was speechless.

"You may go back to your people, Pop-pank," Osh-Tisch said. "But the Shoshone want you to know, the Shoshone are now your people too."

Mayme looked to Muha ai-wa for clarification.

"Osh-Tisch means that you are free to come and go as you like. But if you choose to stay away, he must accept that. But if you choose to stay or come back, he would be very much honored."

Chapter Twenty-two

TWO DAYS LATER, Mayme sat astride Duster and waited as the tribe members filed past, each one patting her on the leg as they went by.

As expected, Muha ai-wa was the last in line.

"I will never forget you, Pop-pank. My friend. My sister." Muha ai-wa lifted a beautifully beaded knife sheath up to her. Muha ai-wa's knife was inside. "I give you this to remember me."

Mayme slid off Duster and took Muha ai-wa in her arms and hugged her tightly. "I will always remember you, my friend, my sister."

Muha ai-wa pulled back, releasing Mayme. "Go now. The sun is still low. You can put many miles under your horse's hooves before it travels to the other side." She turned abruptly and walked into the tepee.

Mayme looked around. It seemed the Shoshone hated goodbyes as they had all disappeared into their tepees. She put her foot in the stirrup and stepped up. She took one look, committing to memory the sights and smells and most of all, the acceptance she'd felt in this tribe.

She knew if she didn't go now . . .

MAYME BATTLED WITH mixed emotions for two days. She thought about what she'd be returning to in the white man's world: A society who hated the Indians despite ignorance of their ways. She travelled with a heavy heart and wondered why she wasn't more excited about the life she'd be going back to.

She didn't know if she wanted to continue working for the post. They had probably hired her replacement long ago anyway. Could she see herself working at the mercantile for the rest of her life? Would her heart and soul not yearn for the mountains? Would her ears not strain to hear the howl of the wolf? Would her flesh adjust to feeling the scratch of a wool blanket instead of the softness of a buffalo hide beneath her? Mayme looked down at her garments: beading decorated her shirt, leggings and moccasins made of the softest material she'd ever worn. She smelled of pine smoke, sunshine, and horse. Perfumes and soap would accost her senses.

She knew she was caught between two worlds. It was up to her to decide which one was the right one for her. The one she would feel right living and dying in. People would look at her differently if she went back. No one would trust her. There'd only be suspicion.

She pulled Duster up short and looked behind her. The sun was beginning to set. An array of reds, blues, yellows, and orange streaked across the sky.

Instead of heading west, she turned Duster in the direction of Oro Fino Creek. She decided to intercept a post rider. She was determined to wait a week if she had to. She would send word to Betty and Mr. Smart that she was alive and well. Maybe someday, when the world was different, she'd take Muha ai-wa to meet both of them.

DUSTER PRICKED HER ears forward and looked toward the east. Mayme stood up from a log next to the river where she'd been waiting. She'd been here for over a week now. Since this spot was the only safe place to cross for miles in either direction, Mayme knew it was only a matter of time before the post rider would come through.

The rattle of shod hooves on the river rock and a splash signified he was close. She held Duster by the reins and walked closer.

The rider pulled up sharply and yelled, "Whoa."

Mayme put her hand up. "I used to be a post rider and this was my route."

"There weren't no girls running post." He eyed her

suspiciously and slid his hand closer to the gun in his holster. Mayme could see his eyes darting around, expecting an ambush.

"I went by the name Nathan Adams. I disguised myself as a boy so I could ride."

The rider jutted his chin at her. "Word had it Nathan got kilt by Injuns. How do I know you're not making this up?"

Mayme studied the boy. Something seemed familiar about him. Was it his brown eyes? Long, slender fingers? Was he carrying a bit too much weight on his hips for a rider?"

"Here." Mayme took the loop of braided horsehair from around her neck. The pocket watch dangled from it. She'd wound it and adjusted the time, although she was amazed that it still worked. "If you would do me this kind favour. Please show Betty . . . I mean Kitty, in Oro Fino, this watch. She will know. I know I'm asking a lot. But if you could keep this ticking and give it to Mr. Smart when you deliver the mail in Eagle Rock, I will ensure you safe passage by the Shoshone."

Mayme didn't know if she could make good on the promise or not. Surely if she talked to Osh-Tisch, he might be agreeable to keeping the post riders safe. At any rate, she needed something to bargain with.

"All right." The boy's face suddenly softened.

Mayme lifted the watch, placed it in the palm of his hand, and studied his face. She smiled devishly. "It's nice not having to shave, but a bugger keeping your hair short enough, isn't it?"

Mayme mounted Duster and threw her head back and laughed. She winked at the rider and reined Duster to the west. She was going home.

Glossary

mochila. A saddlebag designed specifically to carry mail. The mochila had a hole in the front to fit over the saddle horn and a slit for the cantle behind. At the corners were four locked leather boxes where the mail was kept.
hod. A small pail for carrying coal
mogo'ne. woman
nana. man
Ponzo-bert. "Otter Girl"
o-yem-fat-sup. chest or trunk
nuikwi. run
anta. different
ba'nangu. up
ca-tto'aih. to remove
bizi. breast
ca'iju. good, thanks
Osh-Tisch. "finds them and kills them"
yetwitigi. be seated
tckkahpaitseh. invite to eat
natekkat-i. good to eat, edible food
naadoihu. urinate
ah-be-guy. lay down
tukkwan. under, beneath
wemmiha. tired
caan-kammah. to taste good
Osh-Tisch tsategi-nei' aiwa tu hudda. Osh-Tisch has returned with deer
namasuah. get dressed
wookahtea. ask to help (work)
teteaiwoppih. worker/helper
himakka. hold/keep/carry
Muha ai-wa. "Moon Fawn"
we-its. knife

hadug. yes
taipo. white man
Muha ada. "Moon Raven"
eshi eshi. thanks
Pop-pank. "Jumping Fish"
yaakki. bring here

Laurie Salzler holds a degree in Natural Resources Conservation and Outdoor Recreation. She has worked with animals (wild and domesticated) her entire life, including several years spent in the veterinary field and equine industry at training and breeding facilities in New York, Pennsylvania, and Michigan. She is an avid outdoor enthusiast, whose activities include horseback riding, hiking, kayaking, bird-watching, photography, and one of her favourite pastimes, walking with her pack of canines. As a member of WIRES (Wildlife Information, Rescue and Education Service), she is involved in rescuing and rehabilitating native Australian wildlife in New South Wales.